Stardogs,
Book One
Return to Redsky
by
Herbert Grosshans

Published by
Melange Books, LLC
White Bear Lake, MN 55110
www.melange-books.com

Stardogs, Book One *Copyright © 2007, 2011* Herbert Grosshans
ISBN 978-1-61235-019-6

Credits

Editor: Taylor Evans
Copy Editor: Mae Powers
Format Editor: Mae Powers
Cover Layout: A. Bratt

Stardogs - Book One
Return to Redsky
by
Herbert Grosshans

When the Stardogs set up a base on Redsky, the Terran Empire sends Major Griffin and his team of super soldiers to investigate. Griffin has a personal vendetta. If he has to tear open old wounds he will do it to find the men who framed him for a murder he didn't commit.

Herbert loves Science Fiction. He started reading SF as a teenager and soon tried his hand on writing his own stories. His first full length novel 'The Galactics' will remain hidden in the dark recesses of a closet. Before computers, he wrote his stories first in a scribbler and then again on a manual typewriter. He still uses a scribbler, finding it easier than writing on a keyboard. That way he can write anywhere. The computer is the next step, which is also the first editing. His first short story Book One of 'The Xandra' series, Daughter of the Dark, became an instant bestseller. He also wrote and published numerous short stories and a Sci-Fi novel, 'Seeds of Chaos', published as two books, 'Eden's Gate' and 'Hell's Gate'.

Most of Herbert's stories contain Erotica.
Visit Herbert at
http://hegro.blogspot.com

I dedicate this book to Jewel Adams
who gave me a chance and who believed in me.

Check out Herbert's other books and short stories at
www.melange-books.com

The Xandra, Book One, Daughter Of The dark
The Xandra, Book Two, Mother of Light.
The Xandra, Book Three, Goddess of Life.

Dual Visions (Cliffs of Time, Orion -- the Hunt).
Seeds Of Chaos Book One-Eden's Gate.
Seeds Of Chaos Book Two-Hell's Gate.

Short stories:
Orola, The Kiir (Midnight Raunch)
For Love of Arilee (Sweet Challenge)
A Taste of Paradise (Men of Eros, September 2007)

Coming in 2008 at www.melange-books.com
by Herbert Grosshans:

The Stardogs, Book Two, Redemption
Anthology 'Tapestry of Dreams', Eight tales of the Imagination,
Time Flares (Beyond the Stars Digest)
Outpost Epsilon

Stardogs - Book One
Return to Redsky
by
Herbert Grosshans

Chapter One

I looked at the red sun in the sky, and then at the two barely visible small moons hanging low above the horizon. They brought a lump to my throat, and I swallowed hard. It felt good to be home again.

The first twenty years of my life I had spent traveling across the surface of Redsky or *Shantra,* as the natives called this planet. Number five of the twelve circling a Red Giant, 320 light years away from Earth.

Leaving the spaceport behind me, I walked towards Old Town, wondering if anyone would be happy to see me.

Ten years is a long time to be away. Time enough for people to forget, for wounds to heal.

Without conscious thought my hand went up to my face, touched the long, thin line running along the left side of my jaw. Some wounds never heal. Outside maybe, but not inside.

A sudden gust of wind swept along the dirt road, swirling up the yellow dust. I walked slowly. There was no need to hurry.

Above, a Yac-bird circled, looking for prey. I heard its sharp, piercing cry, and it brought back long forgotten memories. Squinting against the fiery red sun, I tried to make out the ridge of the Golgat-mountains in the hazy distance, where I had hunted the fierce *Gaar.* So long ago, and yet...it seemed like only yesterday.

I had walked for nearly an hour, when the drumming of hoofs came from the forest to my left, and I was not surprised to see the small band bursting into the open. They reached me quickly. Their riding animals reared high as they formed a circle around me.

I'd been warned back at the spaceport. *Things have changed a lot here, Griffin. There have been clashes between the settlers and the natives, and once you leave the gates you are on your own.*

The guard at the gate shrugged his shoulders when I showed him my badge. "It's your funeral, Major. I wouldn't go out there by myself. And certainly not on foot. Besides, it's a ten hour walk."

But the guards could not hold me. They had no jurisdiction over me.

Only six surrounded me now. Short, stocky males, with long, narrow, arrogant faces. The tips of their horns were painted red. This meant they had all made their first kill.

"Terra-man," mocked the first one, contemptuously pointing his Ginsa-staff into the sky.

The others laughed with a gurgling, frightening sound.

"Brave Terra-man," said one.

"Or very stupid Terra-man," said another.

I felt the hot, fetid breath of one of the animals in my neck, as its rider tried to crowd me, but I didn't move…not yet.

"We shall eat well tonight," laughed the first one. "He's big. Much meat."

"Maybe tough meat."

They spoke the harsh dialect of the mountain tribes, but I had no trouble understanding them. Once I spent a year among one of the tribes, when I was still a boy, and I learned much of their ways.

They prodded me with the blunt end of their Ginsa-staffs, their yellow eyes watching my reaction, waiting for the moment when I would try to defend myself.

"Are the Sons of the Mountains so weak that they need six *Stallions* to spill the blood of one Terra-man?" I said mildly, keeping my hands low.

Their leathery faces showed surprise.

"The Hornless-one speaks the tongue." He pronounced it in a way that meant *less-than-a man but more-than-a-woman*. A certain respect flickered in their eyes and all but one pulled back their steeds.

"Who are you, Terra-man?" he asked, drawing the three fingers of his left hand across his hairy chest. I had to suppress a smile. This fellow was superstitious. He probably never met a Terran who spoke his language so fluently, since only a few gifted linguists could master the guttural sounds of some of the dialects.

"Beware of the *Night-demon* who walks fearlessly in the guise of a Sky-man," one of them murmured, touching the tips of his horns.

"I am exactly what you see," I said. "A man from Terra." I made the sign that meant *equal to you*.

"Where did you learn to speak our tongue?" he demanded, leveling the barbed end of his staff into my direction.

Realizing it was time for some truth, I touched my lips and my forehead, careful not to make any threatening moves. "Twenty summers ago I lived with the Stag-clan of the Golgat-mountains. I was brother to Threehorn."

One of the others exhaled sharply. "Threehorn!" he exclaimed. "I know of him. He was killed ten, no, eleven summers ago. I was very young still, not a man yet. They say a Terra-man killed him. Nobody really knows."

I winced as memory flooded up, like bile.

He looked at me, his yellow eyes glaring. "Even though you made the truth sign, I say you lie, Hornless-one. No Terra-man would be brother to Threehorn." Looking defiantly at the others, he said, "I say we kill him...now!" With that, he brought down his Ginsa-staff, aiming for my unprotected head.

Anticipating his attack, I moved towards him, while simultaneously reaching for his staff. I knew now these men didn't belong to any clan. They were renegades, outcasts. Each of them wore a clan-ring in his right ear, but they were of different designs.

Earth science and those two years on the double-gravity planet in the Antares-system served me well. They had made me faster and stronger than an ordinary man. These poor devils had no chance against me.

Without effort, I pulled my attacker off his mount, breaking his neck as I did so. Before the others realized what had happened I sat in the saddle of the suddenly abandoned riding-animal and swinging the heavy Ginsa-staff. I drove it through the chest of one of them, at the same time cracking the skull of another with my left fist.

Seeing three of their companions dead in a matter of moments, the others hesitated.

One of them cried out, "He is the *Night-demon* himself, the *Dark Hornless-one*. We are lost."

He turned and sped away, the bristles on his back stiff with fright.

The other two looked after him and spat. "Coward!"

I had given them time to think, not wishing to kill all of them, but they left me no choice. Parrying the thrust of the first one, I kicked him in the head with the blunt end of my staff. He fell backward, right into the point of his companion's barbed weapon, but he was already dead, his face split open by the force of my thrust.

The last one looked at me, his yellow eyes mad with anger and fright. He dropped his Ginsa-staff and reached into his pouch for his blade. "Now I kill you, Sky-demon," he screamed hoarsely and whipped his hand back for the throw.

I burned his head off with my laser. His headless body tumbled off his steed and fell to the ground, without spilling a drop of blood, the wound cauterized by the searing heat. Sheathing the gun, I sighed. What I had done was not exactly legal, since the use of atomic weapons was quite restricted. Forbidden on Redsky.

But then...why take chances. There were no witnesses, anyway. Besides, I didn't have to answer to anybody.

Up in the sky the first vultures were already gathering, eager to get on with the grisly feast. I gave the dead bodies one more glance, then I turned my mount towards Old Town. Without looking back, I kicked my heels into the animal's soft flanks.

"Welcome home," I said to myself. "Nothing has changed."

Chapter Two

They'd built a wall around the newer section of Old Town. The stones were smooth and glazed, the joints fused together with atomic burners. Somebody had ignored regulations. When I reached the massive gate, I found it locked.

I looked for a way to announce myself when it slowly swung open. A guard with a heavy projectile weapon in his hands waved me on and closed the gate behind me.

"We didn't expect you yet," he said, looking me over. "They said you'd be on foot."

"I managed to find transportation," I grinned.

"The Mayor is waiting for you in the town hall," the guard said and pointed at a large, white building, barely visible in the distance.

"Thanks, friend, I know my way around here."

A few people stood outside in their front yards. They gave me curious looks as I rode down the dirt-packed road. Except for the wall, the town hadn't changed much. The streets were still unpaved. I saw a few small air-sleds in front of some of the houses. They looked unused. I could detect a sense of unease in the people watching me.

When I rode past a small tavern I had the urge to stop for a drink, but I rode on. Plenty of time for that later.

The town hall looked the same. They had whitewashed it, but it was still a squat, ugly building.

I walked up the stairs, into the small office of the mayor. Behind the desk, sat a short, chubby girl. She wore a dress two sizes too small, with a low-cut front that left nothing to the imagination.

"Hello, beautiful," I said, winking. "I believe Mayor Margin is expecting me."

She fluttered her painted eyelids and smiled. She did have a beautiful smile and nice teeth. "Go right in, sir."

I couldn't help but grin. They certainly treated me with a lot of respect.

The mayor was a tall, thin man, with a bushy mustache. I'd never liked him. He came out of his chair and started coming towards me, when he suddenly stopped and squinted.

"You!" he exclaimed. "What the hell are you doing here?"

I laughed softly and flopped into one of the upholstered chairs. "You've come up in the world, Castor. Last time I saw you, you were still trying to con people out of their hard-earned credits."

"That's a damn lie, and you know it, Griffin!" he fumed, pointing an accusing finger at me. "If there ever was a conman in this town, it was you!" He stood glaring at me. "What do you want here? Tear open old wounds?"

"If I have to...yes," I said, "but that's not why I came." I paused, relishing what came next. "You have had a lot of problems with the native population. There is talk of war. You asked for help, for a troubleshooter. That's me...the Negotiator from Terra."

The mayor walked back to his desk and sat down heavily. "You?" he said, unbelieving. Then he threw back his head and laughed. "I always knew you were crazy," he gasped, "but this proves it. You...Dan Griffin, drifter, troublemaker, sympathizer with the natives, killer. So now you're the Negotiator! What happened to the real one? Did you kill him?"

Without another word I threw him my special badge, watching his laughter die in his throat. He picked up the badge and dropped it immediately. It was keyed to my brainwaves, and nobody else could touch it for more than a few seconds without ill effects.

"It's authentic," I said.

He stared at me, suddenly looking old. "This whole thing is a mistake. We can deal with it, but the governor insisted, so we agreed. We need someone who is impartial. Why did they send us you?"

"Because I am the only one who can handle this particular problem," I said softly and without malice.

He looked into my eyes. Whatever he saw must have scared the hell out of him. "What did they do to you, Griffin?" he whispered, a shudder running through his body.

"I went to hell and back," I said. "They took me away in chains, they took me apart and they put me back together again...many times. You called me a killer. You're right...that's what I am, except now I have a badge behind me. There are a thousand ways to kill a man, and they taught me every one of them."

"I believe you, dammit!" Margin said, putting his face into his hands. "But why the hell you?"

I shrugged. "Because I'm lucky, I guess."

He looked at me, his face gray. "Whatever you're going to do, leave the past alone. What is done is done. Don't make this personal by looking for revenge. A lot of people could get hurt in the process."

"Are you insinuating I might misuse my powers?"

"That's exactly what I'm saying. You can do anything you want and nobody would question it. And I'm afraid you will. I know you, Dan Griffin."

"Then you don't know me at all!" My voice came out harder than I had intended. "I'm here on official business. They sent me because I was born here. I know the people who live on this planet, the human and the indigenous population. There a reason why you have problems, and it is my job to find it. If in the course of my investigation I have to dig up some dirt, I will. People will get hurt."

Getting up, I walked to his desk and picked up my badge. "Just for your information, my visit here is just a courtesy call to let you know I've arrived. I don't really need to report to anyone. Not even to the Prime Minister. By the way, how is Sir Charles DePratt? Still the pompous asshole, I assume?"

Margin shrugged. "How would I know? He is the Prime Minister, and I think even you should show him some respect. After all, he is the representative of Terra here on Redsky."

I gave him a cruel smile. "As of now I am the highest power on Redsky. I represent the Terran Empire with all its might. You'd be wise to remember that." I laughed. "I guess I'll have to pay him a visit after all. Won't he be surprised to see me?"

"If you're referring to his denial when you pleaded for justice, forget it. He is a busy man, and he has done a lot of good for Redsky. Besides, he probably won't even remember you."

"We'll see." I pocketed my badge. "Now that formalities are behind me I'll have to tend to some private business."

"If you're talking about Lane, I suggest you leave her alone."

"She's still my wife," I said and walked out.

* * * *

I drew some stares from curious neighbors when I rode up to the house. It still looked the same, large and impressive. Her parents had been quite wealthy. Even though they never liked me, they gave us this house as our wedding present.

The gate to the yard stood open, so I boldly rode in. Climbing up the steps, I wondered if she still lived here.

I knocked. Through the opaque window, I could see a shadow coming towards the door and open it.

She looked the way I remembered her. Older, but still very attractive.

"Hello, Lane," I said simply and stepped towards her.

She stood as if struck by a lightning bolt. Her lips were round and she just stared at me.

"Dan?" she cried out, her hands to her face. Then she wheeled and ran back into the kitchen, where she stood staring out the window, her fists clenched to her side.

"Why did you come back?" she whispered. "There is nothing here for you."

"Oh, yes, there is," I said gently, stepping behind her and turning her to face me. "For ten years I couldn't get you out of my mind. Wondering what you were doing. Who you slept with. What bastard held you in his arms. It kept me alive all those years."

I crushed her to me, seeking her lips, but she pushed me away, angrily, tears welling up in her dark eyes.

"Go away, Dan. You have no right to be here!"

"I have every right to be here. You are still my wife, Lane, and I never stopped loving you."

"Our marriage has been annulled, and my love for you died when you killed Garth."

She cried out when I grabbed her shoulders and shook her. "I didn't kill your brother, but you never gave me a chance to explain. Threehorn killed Garth. Your brother raped one of Threehorn's blood sisters. Garth and Threehorn fought to the death, and when I tried to interfere, someone hit me over the head from behind. That's how the Security men found me...lying across Garth's dead body, the knife that killed him in my hand."

I let go of her and sank into a chair.

"But the trial...?" she started.

"What trial?" I cursed. "I was never very popular in this damn town. They condemned me without letting me tell my side of the story, glad to be rid of me." I looked up at her. "You don't believe me? Well, don't feel too bad. Nobody else did, either. I spent one year in a prison-colony on a planet with an atmosphere so poisonous they gave us only six months to survive. I made it. Then they sent me to a planet with nothing but swamp and deep jungle, where you had to be

12

on guard thirty hours a day. I never knew it was possible for so many different kinds of venomous reptiles, insects, and plants to exist. If there is a hell somewhere, I've been there!"

I could see the doubt in her face, as she sat down across from me. "How did you ever survive all that?" she asked with a shaky voice.

I laughed. It sounded ugly in my own ears. "Luck or fate," I said. "I don't know. Five years ago a bunch of government scientists used me for a genetic experiment, and they happened to put me through a lie detector. My charges were dropped, and suddenly I was a free man. But the damage had already been done. I couldn't come back here, not the way I was then, my mind and body all screwed up. They fixed me up, changed me, made me into what I am today."

Her face was deathly white as she stared at her trembling hands. "I'm sorry. I didn't know," she whispered.

A noise from the doorway made me turn, and I watched a little girl burst into the room. She stopped when she saw me and looked at me with large brown eyes, smiling shyly.

"Hello." I smiled at her. "Who are you?"

"I'm Kelly," she said, a little breathlessly, "and who are you?"

"That's Uncle Dan," Lane answered for me, holding a hand out to the little girl. Kelly moved into her mother's arms, still smiling at me.

"This is my daughter," Lane said, stroking the girl's soft hair. I could see tears rolling down her cheeks. "I told you, there is nothing here for you, Dan."

I sat silent for a while, trying to quiet the drums in my head, feeling the gallons of acid churning inside my guts.

"Who?" I finally managed to say, my voice sounding almost normal, except for the sand-frog singing duet with me.

"Castor Margin," she whispered.

I should have guessed. The bastard had always had his eye on her, and with me out of the way, there had been nothing to stop him.

The acid inside my guts turned to ice and was reaching for my heart, yelling murder. I felt the little girl's big brown eyes on me and saw her smile.

"My daddy is a very important man," she said. "Do you know him?"

Looking into her innocent eyes, I could feel the ice melting away. "Yes, I know your daddy, sweetheart," I said, in full control of my emotions now. I reached out and touched her flushed cheeks. This

13

could have been my little girl.

Lane was watching me, knowing what must go on inside me. The tears were flowing freely now. "I think you better leave, Dan," she said.

Nodding, I stood and, without looking back, I walked out.

Chapter Three

Getting drunk never really solves any problems, but it helps to forget.

I had been in *Triton's Tavern* many times, back in the old days, but old Miguel wasn't there anymore. A fat, moonfaced man stood behind the counter, wiping it continuously. His lips seemed to be frozen in a wide grin. He nodded when I walked in, tipping an imaginary hat.

"What'll it be?" he asked, still grinning.

"A bottle of your best and a tall glass," I said. "And some privacy."

"I'm sure you'll find both here, sir," he said, pushing a bottle filled with some murky looking liquid at me.

I took a big gulp and almost gagged. Spitting the stuff on the floor, I grabbed his filthy collar. "I said *your best*, Moonface. If I want to poison myself, I can do it cheaper and less painful. And stop grinning."

"I'm sorry, sir," he whined, trying unsuccessfully to change his expression. "I must have grabbed the wrong bottle."

I gave his collar an extra twist.

"I have some private stock you might want to try," he gagged.

When I released him, he waddled to the back and brought a large golden bottle, which he carefully opened. He poured some into a small glass. "Here, sir, try this. It's the best I have."

I grabbed the bottle and threw some money on the counter. "If it's no good, I'll let you know."

I found a small table in a dark corner. Just what I was looking for. I drank straight out of the bottle, and I had to admit, the stuff wasn't bad. When the bottle was almost empty, I felt much better. On a small stage, a girl with a squeaky voice sang a song about a lost love, and it began to sound pretty good to me.

Even the girl at the table next to mine, who struck me as especially ugly when I sat down, suddenly seemed a radiant beauty. I told her so and made her a proposition, but the man she was with didn't seem to like it. He asked me very politely to apologize, but I told him to mind his own business and go to hell.

He stood up and slowly came over to my table. I am not a small man, but this guy was big, and he seemed very sure of himself. When his fist smashed against the side of my head, it felt as if a sledgehammer had hit me.

Any other time he would never have touched me, but a bottle of liquor slows down a man's reflexes.

Anger flared up inside me, as I fell off my chair. My hand touched the butt of my gun, but a tiny voice in the back of my head stopped me. I realized I was drunk, and I might do something I would regret later.

My special badge gave me immunity from many things, but not from murder. And murder it would be, because this man had no chance against me.

He stood, glaring at me. I managed to stand up, and before he could hit me again, I hit him in the stomach, not too hard, but hard enough to send him reeling back. He bellowed something and came at me again.

That kick against the side of my head had sobered me up a little, and given me a terrible headache. I didn't want to hurt him, after all, I started the fight. Since I couldn't let him get away with it, either, this time I laid it right on the tip of big wide chin.

He looked at me, a puzzled expression on his face, then his eyes glazed over and he fell like a heavy tree.

Before I could get back to my table, somebody grabbed my arm and spun me around. I staggered, reaching for my gun, but a hard voice made me stop.

"One false move and it will be your last one."

The shiny badges on their chests told me they were police. There were two of them. Tall and big. They held scatterguns in their hands.

They looked me over, their expression bored and slightly amused.

"Is that your animal outside?" one of them asked.

I grinned. "Why, you wanna arrest it?"

"He's totally drunk," the other one said.

"Let's see your ID," the first one demanded, still covering me with his weapon.

They felt so secure. Even as drunk as I was, I could have taken them both easily. Slowly I flipped back my cape, revealing the tight black uniform of the *Terran Interplanetary Space Force.* They looked at the big blaster on my hip, then into my smiling face.

I showed them my Special Badge. One of them took it, flipped it open, and then hastily handed it back to me.

"Sorry, sir," he apologized. "We didn't know."

Even though Homeworld was far away, the colonies still feared the mighty Terran Empire.

"The name's Dan Griffin," I said. "I'll be staying for awhile." I had some trouble getting the words out. I looked at the almost empty bottle. "Can I invite you boys for a little drink? Somehow I feel like company."

They shook their heads and turned to walk away.

I sat down, staring at the people around me. Suddenly I realized how silent it had become. "Why don't you people get back to what you were doing," I said. "The show is over."

I waved to the girl who had been singing. "Come, have a drink with me. I need someone to cheer me up."

"I don't drink with drunks," she said and started another song.

"Your loss," I mumbled and poured myself another.

"I'll take that invitation," a soft voice said beside me.

I looked up and into her strange colorless eyes, somehow glad to see her. "I should have known you'd come looking for me," I said. "How'd you find me?"

She laughed, her small teeth shiny pearls behind bright red lips. "You must be drunk, lover, to ask a stupid question like that. Come, it's time to sober up."

Taking my arm, she gently, but forcefully led me outside, where she pushed me into her waiting skimmer. I must have passed out, because the next thing I remember was her pulling off my boots. I was lying on a warm, soft bed. I tried to sit, but gave it up, when the bed started to spin.

She undressed me and pulled the cover over my nude body. Then she slipped out of her own clothes. I tried to focus my eyes on her lovely form, but somehow I seemed to get a double exposure.

"Do you know that you're the most beautiful woman in the Galaxy?" I said, stumbling over the words. "And I mean the whole damn Galaxy."

She laughed and slipped under the covers, pressing her warm, soft body against mine. I remember stroking her firm round breasts and fumbling between her legs. But that's all I remember. I don't know if we made love or if I just dreamed about it. I seem to recall the murmur of her gentle, soothing voice, and there is still the echo of her passionate breathing in my ears, or there seems to be.

I don't know, and when I asked her about it in the morning, she only smiled and shrugged her lovely shoulders. "If you can't remember, you'll never know," she said with a mischievous flicker in her strange eyes. "How's your head?"

"Why did you ask?" I moaned, when suddenly a gang of miners started hammering inside my head.

She handed me a glass of water and a pill. "Here, you'll feel better."

* * * *

"You're a bitch," I told her at breakfast. "A real damn teasing bitch!"

"I love you, too," she laughed throatily, sinking her teeth into a juicy fruit.

I could say things like that to her. She'd kill any other man for less. Her name was *Meadow*. Born on the second planet of a minor system, a large dust ball circling a small bright sun, not quite human and as savage and wild as the beasts that roamed the hot dry plains and high ragged mountains.

Tall and slim, high-breasted and long-limbed, she kept her coppery hair at shoulder length, but liked to pin it back to reveal her pointy ears. Her eyes were the strangest thing about her. The pale iris seemed almost nonexistent.

She was an empath, which meant she could read emotions.

From the first time I laid eyes on her I wanted to climb into the sack with her. A strange attraction I had for her. It was neither love nor lust, it was something else.

Meadow knew about Lane. There isn't much you can hide from someone like her. We had been on three assignments together and shared good and bad times. Our lovemaking was always fierce and passionate. She held nothing back, but expected the same from me.

Looking at me from across the table, she said, "I guess I don't have to ask how everything went."

I shook my head. "I had to find out. But I'll survive."

"I know." Reaching for my hand, she stroked it. Somehow, I had the feeling she was pleased about something. "By the way, while you were walking down memory lane, we did not sit around idle. We've tracked down the Stardogs. They've set up a base about a thousand kilometers north of the spaceport."

She lifted her head, staring into the distance. "Someone is coming," she said. I heard a knock on the door a moment later.

"Come in," I called when she nodded.

The man who entered looked familiar, and then I recognized him. Darl Mitas.

We had been good friends. He wore a uniform with a shiny badge. Smiling, he extended a hand. "It is really you, Dan. Welcome home."

When he saw me look at his badge, he shrugged his shoulders. "This visit is not official, not really."

I grinned and took his hand. "The first person who's actually happy to see me. How have you been, old friend?"

He looked at Meadow, suddenly uneasy. I laughed. He hadn't changed much. He had always been a daredevil, afraid of nothing, but put him in the presence of a beautiful woman and he became a *yarl*...a mouse. We used to call him *Darl the Yarl*.

She gave him a radiant smile and he actually blushed.

"I am Meadow," she said with that somewhat breathless sounding voice of hers. "Any friend of Dan's is a friend of mine."

I felt sorry for him, and also a little bit jealous. He was already hopelessly in love with her.

She walked over to a low divan by the window. I watched as he tried to hide his embarrassment when she stood against the light, her lithe body outlined in the semi-transparent robe she wore. She might as well have been nude.

Hearing the sharp intake of his breath, I gave her an accusing stare, but she ignored it, smiling sweetly at her new admirer. "What is the reason for your visit, Darl?" she asked, sinking into the divan. She crossed her long, slender legs, her robe opened slightly, revealing half of her left breast. She didn't seem to notice, her strange eyes were large and bright as she stared into Darl's face.

Why the hell did she always have to put on such a display?

He blinked, shaking his head, and then he looked at me. "A couple of the boys told me they'd seen you in town last night. I thought I'd come and talk to you." Looking around, he found a chair and sank into it. "I still can't believe it, Dan," he said. "We all figured you dead by now."

"I am not easy to kill." I laughed grimly.

"I know." He stared at me. "They found some dead bodies, natives, or what's left of them. You?"

I nodded. "Couldn't be helped."

"I suspected." He smiled. "Anyway, I'm glad you're alive and well."

Something bothered him.

"Why not tell us what's really on your mind," Meadow said softly.

He looked at her, for the first time seeing her strange luminous eyes. "You're not human," he stated and nodded. "You're right, there is something else." Then, looking at me, "You don't have many friends here, you know. Why did you really come back?"

"Tell him, Dan." Meadow sat up straight and pulled the robe over her breast. "He's alright."

We had been friends, yet...I was reluctant. People change. But I always trust Meadow. She was never wrong. Still, I didn't agree with her methods of screening people. Suddenly I realized something. I was jealous.

When I heard her silvery laughter, I walked over to her and sat down beside her. Gently, she touched my cheek and smiled.

"I'm a fool." I said. Then I looked up at Darl who watched us, not quite understanding. "I guess my presence here is scaring a lot of people."

"Maybe it is. Certain people are wondering about your motives."

"I didn't come here for revenge, if that's what you mean."

He seemed to relax. "Why did you come? Lane?"

I winced when he mentioned her name. Looking at Meadow, I said, "Maybe I have been chasing a memory, a dream, which has ended. No, she was not the reason, just part of it."

"You're not welcome here, Dan. They want someone else."

He didn't know why I laughed. "Don't be stupid, Darl. Do you really think the Empire is interested in your silly border wars? Redsky is not even marked on the trading routes. There nothing here anybody wanted...until now."

"Until now? I don't think I understand."

"We've finally ran into another star-faring civilization, equal to our own. We call them the Stardogs. So far there have been no incidents, not openly anyway, but we've had skirmishes."

"How does Redsky fit in?" His eyes flickered to Meadow, and then back to me.

Meadow answered his question. "They're here. They've been here for some time. We don't know the reason for their presence, and that's why we are here. It's our job to find out what they are doing on Redsky, and stop them, if necessary. An open confrontation that could flare into a full-scale interstellar war must be avoided at all cost. Utmost secrecy is of great importance."

Chapter Four

Located at the mouth of the river *Charad,* the small garrison controlled the river and most of the lake that stretched along the foot of the Golgat mountain ridge. The garrison was never more than a thousand men strong, but their number had been reduced by over hundred through clashes with the natives.

A large number of the men were veterans, too old to do active fighting on more hostile planets, so they had been semi-retired on Redsky, where there had been very little action, until recently. The rest of the Force was made up of local volunteers, most of them young.

The garrison commander was a grizzled old veteran who should have been retired years ago.

"What about the local army?" I asked. "As I recall there were more than ten thousand soldiers stationed at Fort Locust."

"Fifteen thousand, Major. We also have a garrison in Westland and in Northland, with five thousand solders in each one." He smiled slightly. "Our population has grown and we needed to increase the number of soldiers."

"Why?"

The commander sighed. "There is unrest at the eastern border, has been for a number of years. The elder Isram leader is getting too old, and there is talk about a new young leader rising. It is no secret that he would like nothing better than start a Holy War to wipe out the *Nonbelievers*, the natives and all the other *filthy dogs* that don't follow his religion."

"A fanatic rebel," said Meadow.

He nodded. "More than that. He believes he is the *Chosen One*, chosen by the Star Gods to lead his people into glory. He claims to be in contact with the Star Gods who have promised to deliver into his hands the means of winning his Holy War."

He leaned back in his chair and pointed at a map on the wall. "That is only one problem we have. There are reports of a large force amassing south of the Strathon Mountains, about a thousand km north from here. Yellowhorns, Stags, Whitebacks, Desert-Sons. They're all there. They also want to start a Holy War."

I looked at Meadow who nodded slightly. The spot the commander indicated corresponded with the location of what could possibly turn out to be a Stardog base.

"How many soldiers is the Empire sending?" He looked at me expectantly.

"Five," I said.

"Five battalions? Not as many as I would have liked to have, but I guess we'll manage."

I couldn't suppress a chuckle. "I didn't say five *battalions*, Commander. I said five."

"Five companies, then?"

"No." I smiled. "Five men."

"Surely you jest, Major." His knuckles turned white when he gripped the wooden arms of his chair.

"He is serious," remarked Meadow.

"Just five men?" he whispered hoarsely. "But why? Are we so unimportant?"

Somehow, I felt sorry for him. "We are not *just five men*, Commander Ryker."

"We are the best the Empire has ever produced, a new breed of soldiers. Each of us capable of defeating an army."

He looked at me and laughed. "Don't try to humor me, Major Griffin. I may be an old man, but I am not senile, nor am I a fool."

I lifted a crystal sphere from its holder on his desk and balanced it on the palm of my right hand. Slowly I closed my fingers around it and crushed it into a heap of broken fragments. His eyes grew wide, and then he shrugged. "I've known strong men before, men who came from high gravity planets. That still doesn't make you a superman."

"Dan Griffin was born on Redsky," said Meadow softly. "His body has been changed in many ways. Besides his incredible strength, he can move faster, jump higher, and throw missiles farther and with more accuracy than any ordinary man. A number of devices have been surgically implanted in his body and connected to his nervous system to make him a walking weapon. To say that Dan Griffin is one of the most dangerous men of the Galaxy is almost an understatement. He is, in fact, the most dangerous man alive."

Commander Ryker stared into her luminous eyes. "And you, Miss?" he asked.

"Me?" She laughed cheerfully, crossing her legs. "There is nothing special about me."

"I'll bet," he murmured, breaking eye contact and looking at me. "I'm almost inclined to believe her. We'll see."

I studied the map behind the commander. There were nineteen small red flags on pins stuck into its surface, marking the spots where fighting had occurred. One of them had the number thirty-nine printed on it.

The commander noticed me looking at it and sighed heavily. "That was a month ago. The men were making a routine check of the outpost by the Tokai-Tempa River-crossing, two hundred kilometers west of here. As you probably know, Major, the territory north of the Tokai-river has always been a trouble spot. In addition to the hostile Fire-Eaters, it is populated by renegades and bandits. My men were ambushed by a band of natives over three hundred strong. We lost thirty-nine good soldiers, only eleven managed to flee, five of them severely wounded."

I didn't have to ask how a bunch of savages could wipe out such a large force of trained soldiers. The answer to that I knew myself. Redsky was designated a 'Class D' planet. Atomic weapons were forbidden. Only projectile weapons were allowed on a 'Class D' planet, and even there were restrictions. No rapid-fire guns or rifles, no canons, no rocket launchers, no bombs. The list was practically endless.

The reason for this was quite simple. If advanced weapons fell into the wrong hands, they could change the delicate balance of power on these primitive planets and create great havoc, causing the death and slaughter of many innocent beings.

Unfortunately, this policy was not easy to adhere to, and there were plenty of men without scruples who would sell anything to anybody, and this included weapons.

The commander opened a drawer in his desk and took out something. Handing it to me, he commented, "We took this from one of the natives killed by our patrols. I've never seen anything like it before."

It was a weapon, but not one Earth science had produced. Shaped like an egg with three indentations at one end, it didn't really look like a gun. It fired small pellets at high velocity. The pellets exploded on contact, making this innocent looking little thing very effective and deadly.

I knew where it came from, but I didn't tell him.

"This weapon comes from off-planet," the commander said, "and I'd like to know who smuggled it to Redsky." He stared at me. "Somehow it doesn't seem to fit into a Human hand."

"You're right." I'd changed my mind. He had a right to know. "It doesn't. It belongs into a three fingered hand with a long opposing thumb."

"You seem to know more than I."

"It seems that way, doesn't it? Well, I guess there is no harm in telling you. We call them the Stardogs, and it looks like they've done already more damage than we hoped."

Chapter Five

Old Town was not only populated by New Wave settlers, but also by settlers who had come to Redsky a thousand years ago, when Humanity first reached the stars. These early colonists lost all contact with their home world Earth. When their machines broke down and began to deteriorate, they soon reverted to barbarism. They spread across Redsky, and when the New Wave settlers arrived, they considered these early colonists natives, along with the indigenous people.

Most people shunned the section of Old Town that was populated by natives and regarded as slums. I spent much time there in my early years and knew most of the streets and lanes. Many of my friends lived there, including San Deloose.

Looking at the weathered sign above the shop's entrance, I wondered if he was still around. When I pushed open the door, I walked into the past. The long forgotten aroma of boiled *tekka-leaves* wafted into my nose and, there behind his old wooden counter, sat a familiar figure.

He looked up. Staring at me, his eyes grew large, and the gray bushy eyebrows danced the way I remembered. His thick mustache quivered when he broke into a toothless grin and, roaring, he came out of his chair.

"Dan Griffin!" He almost sobbed and embraced me, pounding my back. "They told me you were dead." He peered into my face, tears rolling down his wrinkled cheeks.

"I'm very much alive, San." I grinned. "You know me, nothing ever got me down. But I'm glad you didn't forget about me."

"Never, son, never!" He wiped a large hand across his nose. Still staring at me, he said, "You've changed. Your face looks the same, but gone is that carefree look, the 'I don't care about anything' attitude, that certain sparkle in your eyes. I see a man who has lost his innocence. Your eyes mirror the chill inside you, Dan Griffin, and if we were enemies, you'd scare the hell out of me."

"It's been a long time, San, old friend," I said. "People change."

"You must have been in hell to change this much."

How perceptive he was.

He shuffled back to his counter, the way he always had, and poured black steaming liquid into a large mug. "Here," he said and handed it to me. "Let's drink to old times."

"To old times," The hot, bitter drink stung my throat, but it tasted good. Looking around, I had the eerie feeling time had stood still in this place. The same old racks held the same looking clothing that had been there ten years ago. On the shelves stood familiar pottery in all kinds of shapes and sizes. The walls were cluttered with tools and other utensils. Things that one could get only in this section of Old Town.

San Deloose and I, we went back a long time. He had been a friend of my father's and, after my parents were killed, he more or less took care of me until I could look after myself. He owned a small shop, buying and selling anything he could get his hands on, and he was not too concerned where it came from or who bought it. His ancestors had been among the first settlers.

Many times he took me into the mountains to deal with the mountain-tribes, and when he went to jail for a year, he left me with the Stag-clan, whose young chief Threehorn took a liking to me.

We sat for hours and talked. I did most of the talking. San was a good listener, and he seemed to enjoy my tales of the strange planets I had visited. I tried to keep it on the light side and talked only of the beauty I had seen, but somehow the terror always seemed to creep back into my stories.

He just sat there and listened, sipping from his mug, and when there finally was nothing more to tell, he looked at me for a long time, his black eyes grave. "You didn't deserve this, son. No human being should be treated the way they treated you. They can never give back what they took from you, no matter how much power they give you. You don't owe them anything. Why not forget about the Empire and stay here?"

I shook my head, smiling. "I have a job to do, San, and believe it or not, somehow coming back here has given me a new purpose in life. I don't think I belong here anymore. Like you said, I've changed."

He nodded, sadly, "I'm not sure if for the better. There is more to living than just doing a job. What about that rich girl you married? What does she think about all this?"

"We've split. She married someone else." I shrugged, surprised how calm I sounded.

"Maybe it's just as well. I never thought she was right for you. You grew up in a different world from hers."

"I did love her and she loved me, once," I said softly.

He padded my shoulder, the way he had always done when he wanted to console me. "I had a woman who loved me. A long time ago. She left me for a younger man when I took her with me into the North-countries. Just took off one night." He chuckled. "Tell you the truth, she was a nag, never happy. I hope she found what she was seeking. Never heard from her again."

It was dark when I left his shop, carrying a large bundle with things I needed. I loaded it onto the animal I had tied to a tree. Slowly, I walked down the dark narrow street, pulling the animal behind me.

It was not very smart to travel through this section of town after dark, and it didn't take long before I heard footsteps behind me. I knew there were four of them, three men and one woman. The sound of her bare feet was easily distinguishable from the heavier footsteps of the three men. One of them big, he shuffled as he walked on heavy feet.

They circled me from behind, the woman gliding by me on my left under cover of some small shrubs. Two of the men were on either side of me now, slightly hanging back, while the third one stayed behind. He carried a heavy club. I could hear the faint scraping as he rubbed it with his left hand.

My built-in defense system had shifted my body in combat-mode. Tiny implants all over my body let me sense and hear things a normal Human could not.

The woman stepped into the street in front of me. "What's your hurry?" she asked, parting her cape. She wore nothing underneath. She was young, a girl with the body of a woman, her breasts high and full; two solid fleshy cones with dark nipples jutting from her ribcage. She could have been beautiful, if it hadn't been for her straggly hair and her calculating eyes. This was no innocent girl. She had seen and done more things than a girl her age should have.

The pale light from one of the moons shone down the length of her slim nude body, revealing the dark triangle below her flat belly.

"Well?" she said, smiling. "Do you like what you see?"

As she came closer, I could hear the man with the club moving in behind me. The other two were still hidden in the darkness of the houses, but I heard the barely audible whispering sound of a long knife being pulled from its sheath

She stood close enough now to touch, and I could smell the odor of her body. A bath was long overdue. Both of her front teeth were missing.

Lifting her arms, she jiggled her breasts. The cape slid off her shoulders, leaving her completely nude. She stepped back slightly, but it had not been necessary for me to see the flicker in her eyes.

As the club descended, my free right arm shot up, deflecting the murderous blow and, with the same movement, my fist connected with the side of the club-wielder's head, sending him sprawling into the dirt. I hadn't killed him, but he would be out for some time.

The man with the knife rushed me from the right, the other one stayed invisible behind my steed. I could tell my attacker was an amateur. He held the knife in front of him, his knife arm stiff. An experienced street fighter would never do that. I grabbed his wrist and broke his arm. He screamed and cowered back, holding his injured limb.

Now the last of them stepped around the animal, carrying a heavy axe.

"You fight well," he rumbled, grinning, his wide chin pointing towards the two on the ground, "against children."

He was right, the other two were young, but I knew that already. That's why I hadn't killed them.

He hefted his axe. "Let's see how you fare against a man."

* * * *

Big and desperate, that made him a dangerous opponent, but he was also a fool. Because he saw an unarmed man, he became careless and overconfident.

"You've hurt my boys," he said. "I think for that I'll kill you." He drew a circle with his left finger.

Chuckling, I signed the figure eight in the air, then I spat twice onto the ground.

His eyes narrowed and he hesitated. "Your clothes say you're a Terran, but your manner says different."

"I am a Terran," I said, "but I am also Shantra." I used the native word for *Redsky*.

He became cautious now. "You talk in riddles, but you speak our language well. Maybe you're a spy."

"I am no spy," I said, getting tired of the conversation. I made a rude sign with both hands. "Take your boys and the girl and leave me alone, before I loose my patience."

Back at *Solar Intelligence,* they told me that the thing, which made me so dangerous, was my mind, but it also happened to be my weakness. Too closely connected to my heart. They had made me into a killer, an assassin, but they couldn't make a cold-blooded murderer out of me.

Meadow called me *the most dangerous man alive* and she may have been right...to a degree. I didn't enjoy killing, never have, and someday I would hesitate just a bit too long.

The heavy axe whirled through the air. I moved aside, evading it easily. I heard an ugly thud behind me as the weapon sank into something soft and yielding. I didn't have to look to know what he hit, but it still tore through me when I heard the terrible scream of a creature in agony.

He cursed and tore his axe free. The animal fell to the ground, blood spewing from the horrible cleft the blade left in its shoulder. It kicked a few times, coughed, and lay still, the long black tongue lolling between its bared teeth.

"I liked that animal," I said softly.

He gave an ugly laugh and kicked the carcass. "I'll make you join it shortly, big man." Advancing again, he swung the bloody weapon in an arc over his head.

Even though he had made me angry, I still hesitated. I saw the girl rushing over to the dead animal and untie the bundle it carried. She looked up. "Let him go, Cherco," she called. "We've got what we want."

"I haven't. I'm going to kill this arrogant spawn of a swamp worm, and now shut up!"

He had me backed against the wall and, shouting, he chopped down. It clanked loudly and sparks flew when the metal blade scraped along the rough stones. As the weapon hit the ground, I kicked hard and broke the long heavy handle, leaving only a short piece of splintered wood in his hands.

He looked stunned for a moment, then he jabbed the broken handle towards my face. "I'll crush you with my bare hands if necessary," he growled when I ducked and the broken handle smashed into the stone wall.

I rammed my fist into his stomach. He groaned and doubled over, clutching his belly. His fat neck presented a fair target and I chopped down hard. He collapsed without another sound.

The girl looked at me, her eyes large with sudden fright when I walked over to her. "He's alive," I said, taking the bundle from her numb hands.

Her cape, which she had put on again, had fallen open, exposing her naked body, but she didn't seem to be aware of it. For the first time I noticed the scars and bruises covering her body.

"I don't really care," she said vehemently. "You should have killed him. He's evil."

"He beats you?"

She spat. "That and other things. I hate him."

"Why don't you leave him?"

"And go where? I have nobody. He's the only family I ever had, and he feeds and protects me."

"Is he your father?"

She shook her head. "No. My father is dead. So is my mother."

I shrugged. I felt sorry for her, but there wasn't much I could do. "You're lucky I didn't kill him, then," I said and turned to go.

She ran after me and grabbed my arm. "Take me with you," she pleaded. "You're strong and could provide for me. I'd do anything for you." She smiled. "I could give you much pleasure. I'm young, but I have lots of experience in the ways of coupling. You can have me right now, if you want. Please?" Again, she spread her cape, displaying her nude body to me.

A door suddenly flew open beside us, and a man stepped out. He carried a lantern in one hand and a long knife in the other. He looked first at me, then at the girl's exposed body. His eyes narrowed, he turned around and said something to someone behind him. After he moved away from the door, two more men joined him. They looked at the girl and grinned.

"Are we invited to this party?" one of them asked.

The girl clutched my arm. "Let's run," she said in universal. "They'll kill you, and then they'll take me to the slave market. I'd rather die before I become a slave."

I gave the newcomers the once-over. I could tell they were not locals by the way they dressed. Probably travelers or traders who had come with one of the caravans from the north.

"Let's kill the starman and get the girl. She's obviously *garan* and won't be missed. She should fetch a good price." The speaker grinned and made a sign with his left hand. The others laughed. The girl had been right. They had called her *garan*, a 'prostitute without protection', and therefore considered her fair game. They also meant to rape her.

"Terra-man," one of them sneered in universal, "did you come looking for adventure? Something different perhaps? Or are there no women in your part of town who wish to perform for you?"

"Actually, I came looking for men, but all I see is *jelcos*," I said. I saw the anger flare up in their faces. I had called them *skunks who rape dead old women*. Because I spoke universal, I had to restrain myself from making the appropriate signs, which was too bad. It would have been like rubbing salt into an open wound.

While we talked, the second moon came up and took away some of the darkness. The bodies of the unconscious men on the road behind us were clearly visible in the somewhat greenish light. The guy whose arm I had broken seemed nowhere in sight.

"The Starman has been busy. Perhaps we should be more cautious."

Behind the three a forth man appeared. He had a dark, scowling face, and he carried something in his hand. Instantly I became alert.

"A Terra-man!" he cursed when he spied me and casually leveled the pencil-shaped object in my direction.

The moment I registered the slight narrowing of his eyes I realized it was too late to be polite. Pushing the girl away from me, I dropped and rolled, at the same time drawing my blaster. The blast of hot air washed over me the instant I heard the crackling on the wall behind the spot I had been standing.

I shot him while I still rolled. Coming up beside the one with the knife, I rammed my stiffened fingers into his throat, killing him almost instantly. The other two looked at me and at the blaster in my hand, then they turned and ran.

I pried the small laser from the dead man's hand and pocketed it.

"Let's go," I said to the girl who watched me with large eyes. I smiled at her. "I'll protect you."

She sighed and smiled back at me.

Walking ahead, I activated the transmitter built into my upper palate with my tongue. Almost instantly, as if she had expected the call, Meadow answered my signal. "What's up, Dan?" Her voice sounded like a whisper in the receiver behind my ear, but clear and audible.

"I need transportation, Meadow." I spoke quickly. "Come and pick me up."

"I'll be there shortly, Dan. I have a fix on your position."

About fifteen minutes later, she dropped her skimmer into the street in front of us. She lifted an eyebrow when she saw my companion. "Going after the young girls now, lover?"

The girl seemed reluctant to enter the skimmer, but I pushed her gently into the backseat, stowed my pack beside her and sank into the seat next to Meadow. "I promised her protection. Take us home and give her a good meal and a long, hot bath. She needs it."

Meadow smiled, her white pearly teeth shining between red lips.

"And get her teeth fixed," I added. "I have something against women with rotten teeth."

She took the skimmer up and leveled it. Looking at me, she said softly, "Something is troubling you." I showed her the pencil-shaped laser. "Earth-made," she said.

"Yeah. Tell me, what is it doing on a Class D planet?"

Chapter Six

The seat of the local government was located in Capital City, the largest city in Newland. Small, when compared to the cities on Terra, which were overcrowded with buildings and people, but large for Redsky.

Capital City sprawled across a vast area, like most cities on Redsky. Nobody believed in crowding buildings too close together. The highest building rose five stories high. According to the statistics, 175,000 people called Capital City home. Correction...had called it home, because my information lagged ten years behind. I made a mental note to look it up in the database.

The city was divided by the *Blue River*, which ran right through its middle. A tributary to the *Blue River*, called *Fast River*, cut the western part of the city almost in half.

Prime Minister Sir Charles DePratt and his lovely wife Lady Evana lived on the fifth floor of Government House, the building that housed the government offices. It also happened to be occupied by the *High Court of the Land*, a place much too familiar to me.

"Painful memories?" Meadow asked. She knew, but she asked anyway.

I nodded, smiling. "Nothing I can't deal with."

She touched my hand briefly. You can't fool an empath.

The guards at the entrance to Government House saluted smartly when I walked up the wide steps. Dressed in my black tight fitting uniform and my cape open, to display the insignia of the Empire on my chest, I knew I looked impressive. The high black boots added to the symbol of power I represented, even though they were as uncomfortable as hell.

I entered the building with grim satisfaction.

"Major Griffin of the Terran Interplanetary Space Force to see

Prime Minister DePratt," I told the attendant at the front desk.

He made a big show of checking his guest book, and then he looked up and smiled. "I will announce you, sir," he said with a nasal voice and pushed a button on his intercom. Nothing seemed to happen, because he suddenly had this blank look on his face, then he fumbled with the wires that ran from the unit on his desk into one of the drawers. Looking up at me, he said, "Just give me a moment until I fix this, sir. It's the latest in communication, but there are still a few bugs that need to be worked out."

I had to suppress a smile. What he called *latest in communication* was something not even children played with on Terra and the planets nearest to Homeworld. Being a Class D planet, it would take Redsky a long time to get really sophisticated stuff.

Electricity, for instance, was still produced by generators. There were a number of waterfalls in the Fast River, strong enough to run giant turbines, one of the reasons Capital City had been build at this location. Most of the small towns didn't have electricity. They still used vegetable oil for light and wood for heating.

"Take your time," I said. "We're in no hurry."

Meadow lacked my patience. Sighing, she reached out and plugged the wire from his headset into the unit. "Try it now," she said, giving me an innocent smile.

She looked stunning in her yellow dress. Tight and formfitting, it left nothing for speculation about her figure. She had her coppery hair pulled back, but it wasn't really necessary to see her pointy ears to know she was not human.

The attendant pretended to notice her for the first time. "Thank you, my Lady," he mumbled, avoiding looking into her pale eyes. There were still a lot of people, even here on Redsky, who would not acknowledge that there were other intelligent races besides humans.

He looked at me. "You'll have to leave your weapons down here, sir," he said with an apologetic shrug and smiled crookedly. "Regulations, you know."

"No problem." I unbuckled my belt and gave it and the blaster to him.

The poor arrogant, ignorant fool! What need has a soldier of the Empire for a weapon? My whole body was a weapon.

"Please, follow me, Major Griffin," said a woman's voice beside me. I turned to look at her. She was young, tall, and quite pretty. She smiled at me. "I am Temarra." She hooked her arm into mine. "Come, my father is waiting."

We took a private elevator up to the fifth floor.

"I hear you've just arrived from Terra," Temarra chatted. "I've never been there myself. I was born here on this *godforsaken planet*, as my mother calls Redsky. She'll be excited to talk to someone who's been there recently. She was born there, you know. So was my father."

I smiled at her. "I know."

"I don't think I'd like it there. Too many people." She looked up at me. "How do you like our planet so far?"

"Better than Terra," I said, amused by her youthful enthusiasm. It was obvious, she hadn't been told anything about me.

Another armed guard waited for us as we stepped out of the elevator. He nodded towards Temarra, ignored me completely, but gave Meadow a curious stare, his eyes all but devouring her body.

I couldn't blame him. She did look delicious.

Temarra took us down a long corridor, stopped in front of a wide door. Before she opened it, she smiled at me. "My father's position as governor carries certain privileges. Most people on Redsky don't live the luxurious way we do."

Unhooking her arm from mine, she opened the door and walked in ahead of us. We entered a large vestibule. The luxury Temarra had been talking about was clearly evident. Large chandeliers hung from the ceiling, oil paintings on the walls, some of them imported from Homeworld. Cabinets and tables hand-carved by local artisans, chairs and couches covered with leather, rugs made from the skins of Redsky's numerous predators; they all testified to the wealth of Prime Minister Sir Charles DePratt.

A number of people stood in front of a large window, holding slim glasses in their hands.

A tall woman wearing a long black dress with a deep décolleté that displayed her prominent breasts spotted us as Meadow and I slowly walked into the room. She smiled and came to greet us.

"This is Major Griffin and his friend," Temarra introduced us. Turning to me, she said, "This is my mother, Lady Evana."

I made a bow towards the woman. "I am pleased to meet you, my Lady. By the way, this is Meadow."

Lady Evana glanced at Meadow. "Nice to meet you."

"I'm sure you are," Meadow said in this sweet voice that she used when irritated. "I've been looking forward to finding out how rich civilians live on these backwater planets."

"Like this," Lady Evana said with a sweeping gesture. "But my husband isn't just a civilian. After all, he is the Prime Minister. Or didn't you know?" She looked at me. "Your escort isn't on the guest list. Who is she?"

"I am a lieutenant with the Terran Interplanetary Space Force," Meadow answered for me.

"Oh, how interesting. I wasn't aware that the Terran military recruited members from an alien species."

"I guess you've been stuck here for too long on this...how do you call Redsky? This *godforsaken planet*? Things have changed a lot on your Earth." Meadow's pale eyes almost glowed under her delicately arched eyebrows. She made it a habit of rubbing certain people the wrong way, part of her strategy to read them more easily.

If Lady Evana was aware of Meadow's little game, she didn't show it. She laughed. "You are probably right. It's been a long time." She took my arm, dismissing Meadow with this simple gesture. "Come, Major, I will introduce you to our other guests."

Sir Charles DePratt was an imposing man. Almost as tall as my 190 cm, big and bulky, especially around his middle, and quite bald. Back on Homeworld, his baldness could have been treated. Here on Redsky, he had to live with it. "So you are the famous Major Griffin," he greeted me jovially, his handshake firm and strong. "A genuine pleasure to meet you."

Castor Margin had been right. He didn't remember me. And I wasn't going to enlighten him. Not yet.

His eyes looked past me. I knew, of course, what or who he looked at. "Introduce me to his lovely young lady."

"This lovely young lady is Lieutenant Meadow Rainseeker...my aide."

I saw the look Lady Evana threw him when he took Meadow's hand and kissed it. "She's an alien," she pointed out.

The Prime Minister smiled, his eyes casually studying Meadow. "It's hardly obvious," he said. "I find those pointy ears rather exotic. Otherwise she looks human." He offered Meadow his arm. "Come, I'll show you around." With a look at his wife, "I'm sure the Major has many amusing stories to tell about Terra."

I had to grin. If he had any plans for Meadow, he was going to be disappointed. He might get a kick in the balls for his efforts, but nothing else.

However, Meadow would find out a lot about Prime Minister Sir Charles DePratt.

There were three other couples. One young, the other two older. One of the older men, a short, rotund man with a small goatee, looked familiar. Then I remembered him.

Judge W. G. Wambaugh.

The man who had condemned me to life in a prison colony. The man who had rushed my trial without giving me a chance to defend myself.

"You look like someone I've seen before," he said when I shook his hand.

I smiled. "You have, your Honor. Ten years ago. In your courtroom."

"I don't understand."

"The trial of Dan Griffin, who was accused of murdering Garth Oshinsky, the brother of Mayor Castor's wife Lane, formerly Mrs. Griffin...my wife."

His little pig's eyes became even smaller when he peered into my face. "I remember that trial. It was an open-and-shut case. The Prime Minister even told me not to waste too much time on it. I gave that man a life sentence. You can't be him. He was a criminal, a murderer. How could you be him? You are playing a cruel joke, Major."

"No joke." I enjoyed this little game. "A higher court found me innocent, a court that listened to me."

"Does that mean you're a native of Redsky?" Lady Evana asked beside me.

"That's correct," I said. "Born and raised on Shantra." I used the native word for Redsky deliberately.

"But I thought you came from Terra?"

"I spent some time there, if only briefly. Most of the time I practiced warfare." I smiled at her. "You won't believe the things I have seen."

Even though she wasn't that young anymore, time had been kind to her, leaving her face unlined and her skin smooth. Only a few wrinkles around her eyes and a net of fine lines crisscrossing her neck betrayed her age. In a way, I felt sorry for her. She had once been a beautiful young woman, full of life, eager to follow her husband to a new, exciting planet. Now she found that she wasted the prime of her life on a primitive planet, away from the glamour and richness of the civilized worlds.

Her dark eyes studied me with a deeper interest. "You must tell me about these things," she said. "Tell me about Earth." She pulled me towards one of the low couches, told me to sit down and went to get us a drink.

Judge Wambaugh had followed us. Standing in front of me, he said, "I did nothing wrong. I only did what I was told."

I felt coldness inside me when I looked at him. It must have shown in my eyes, because he seemed to shrivel inside his fancy suit. "Who ordered you what to do?" I asked.

He didn't get a chance to answer. Lady Evana returned with the drinks and smiled at the judge. "Excuse me, Walter, but I'd like to claim the Major for myself, just for a short time."

* * * *

"Are you and that alien woman lovers?" Lady Evana looked at me over the rim of her glass, her dark eyes hidden behind the veil of her lowered lashes.

Standing in front of her as she sat on the edge of the bed, I had an excellent view of her breasts, and there was a lot to see. When I didn't respond to her question, she smiled. "You don't have to answer that. It's none of my business." She opened her eyes wide and stared at me. "You know what I want from you, don't you?"

"I think I do," I said, cautiously. After all, she was the Prime Minister's wife. I couldn't afford to misread her signals, as clear as they seemed to be.

She put her empty glass on the floor and reached for me. Very casually, while looking up at me with a mischievous smile on her full lips, she opened my belt and slowly pulled down my zipper. Already hard and straining, my *Number One* didn't need any coaxing to make an appearance.

"Oh my," she said, licking her lips. "He certainly isn't shy."

I laughed, watching her take my erect member into her mouth. Her velvety tongue began go move around the swollen head with circular motions, and with tantalizing slowness, she sucked me deeper into her oral cavity.

Not many women can swallow a whole penis, most of them will gag, but Lady Evana didn't have such a problem. Moving her head leisurely back and forth, she almost made me come, but she freed me before I exploded inside her warm mouth.

"Get undressed!" she told me softly, while undoing the top of her dress and pushing it down past her hips. Her breasts tumbled out, surprising me with their firmness. "Come on, hurry up." She let the dress pool on the floor and pulled up her legs to expose her hairy pussy. I realized she didn't wear any panties. As if reading my thoughts, she chuckled. "I knew you were coming, so I was prepared."

My smart-looking boots gave me a bit of trouble, but I managed to pull them off my feet without tripping over my pants. Then I sank to my knees and put my face between her spread legs. Inhaling the musky scent of her pussy and the perfume she had sprayed onto her genital area, I pulled open her pussy-lips and pushed my tongue into the pink cleft.

She moaned deeply and grabbed my head. "Yes...that's it!" she cried out and let her legs fall open "That's it...oh...yes..."

Taking her rigid clitoris between my teeth, I gently sucked on it, making her cry out so loud, I expected an armed squad storming into the bedroom.

"Don't stop," she sobbed when I lifted my head for a moment to grab some air. Her long fingers were entangled in my hair, and she pulled my face back between her legs. "Please, don't stop."

My member was hard and demanded more than just standing at attention, so after awhile I slid on top of her soft, yielding body. When I entered her, she let out a deep, loud moan and pushed up against me. "Don't hurry," she gasped. "Just don't hurry."

I fucked her slowly and with deep thrusts, and I had to close her mouth with mine to muffle her cries of pleasure every time she experienced an orgasm.

"Don't pull out when you come," she whispered, after calming down from a particular high climax. She was beginning to tire and I knew I had to end it soon.

"Alright," I grunted and let the built-up pressure inside me bubble to the surface. "Now!" I called out. My pole began to throb and then I felt it jet into her. She cried out and dug her fingers into my clenching buttocks. I buried my face between her breasts to stifle my own loud moans of pleasure. The inside walls of her pussy quivered around my spurting shaft and milked it forcefully.

I collapsed onto her soft, heaving breasts and lay inside her cradling arms and thighs, happy and content.

"You have no idea how badly I needed this," she said and chuckled. "And neither did I."

I disengaged myself from her embrace and rolled onto my back beside her. "You weren't the only one who needed a good fuck," I said and turned my head to look at her.

She laughed. "A good fuck," she repeated and let her fingers trail across my chest. "I'm not used to such vulgar talk, but it makes me horny all over again." She covered my chest with kisses. "You taste salty," she murmured, licking my skin.

Her hand cupped my balls and squeezed them gently. Slowly her fingers curled around my hardening organ. I could feel her hot, slippery pussy as she rubbed it against my hip. She moaned and moved on top of me. Her soft thighs captured my hard rod. Gasping, she lifted her hips, grabbed my shaft and guided it back into her satiny sheath.

She pushed her upper body away from me, letting me enjoy the view of her swinging breasts above me. Watching my member disappear in the thick carpet of her pubic hair, I felt the soft, creamy walls of her pussy molding around my hard pole.

"Just lie still," she moaned, "let me play a little."

She began snapping her pelvis, slowly at first, then faster, as her orgasm approached. "Here it comes again," she sobbed and quivered on top of me. I cupped her soft buttocks, pulled her into my lap and pushed as far as possible into her, coming at the same time as she did. My grunts of pleasure blended with her soft mewling cries.

She collapsed into my arms and lay gasping against my chest. "I wish I could go on," she murmured after awhile, "but I'm exhausted."

She slid off me. "We'd better get back to my other guests. They may be wondering where we are. You can tell me all about your adventures, before my husband is finished showing your alien friend around." She put a finger between her breasts. "But first I must take a quick shower, I'm sticky all over. You go on ahead. I won't be long."

While I dressed, I watched her walk towards the bathroom. She had nice, full buttocks. Not bad for a woman her age.

* * * *

If any of the other guests had missed us, nobody made a comment when I walked back into the room. The four couples standing by the window just glanced at me and went back to their conversations. Lady Evana joined us only a short time later. She had changed into a different dress, still black, but one that covered her chest.

She smiled at me, as she handed me a glass. "I thought you might want to have a fresh drink."

It seemed Prime Minister DePratt had been a gentleman after all. He and Meadow were both laughing at some private joke, when they returned to join us for dinner.

Lady Evana, looking prim and proper, asked me politely to sit beside her. I had to suppress a smile. She was quite an actress. Nothing to indicate that only a short time ago she had been whimpering and clawing at my body as she released her pent-up passion. Even her make-up looked untouched.

The Prime Minister looked at me from across the table. "You are a fortunate man, Major Griffin," he said jovially.

"How so?"

"To have a devoted woman like Lt. Rainseeker as an aide. She thinks very highly of you."

Meadow laughed and touched his arm in a gesture much too familiar for my taste. "Don't give away any secrets, Sir Charles. That information was for your ears only."

Sir Charles DePratt chuckled and put a hand over his mouth. "Oh, oh. I'd better be careful. As the head of the government I can't afford to let secrets leak to the public." He winked at me. "She would be a great addition to my police force. She has a gift for extracting information, without you being aware of it. I could use someone like her." Turning back to Meadow, he asked, "How about it?"

Meadow smiled. "Thank you. I'm flattered, but I already have a job."

"See what I mean?" The Prime Minister laughed and said, with a glance at Lady Evana, "Actually, I already have someone who is quite efficient at getting information." He looked at his wife. "Did you manage to get anything useful out of the Major?"

"I'm not sure how useful. We've spent a couple of interesting hours, though. Major Griffin has led a fascinating life, if everything he told me is true. If not, then he is an amusing storyteller."

"I might have stretched the truth a little, I admit." I chuckled. "Not everything I've experienced was amusing." I never told her anything about my life on Redsky, about the great time with the Stag-clan, about my friendship with Threehorn, about his sister Blue Petal. Or about my marriage to Lane.

"Why exactly did you come to Redsky, Major Griffin?"

The question came unexpected. "Because you requested it, Prime Minister."

He shook his head. "I didn't. It was Governor Delhouse's idea.

He and Commander Ryker are blowing this whole situation with the natives out of proportion. We could have handled it ourselves."

"I spoke with Commander Ryker. He doesn't think so." I didn't tell him the real reason we were here. Maybe he knew about the Stardogs, maybe not. I didn't trust the man. I didn't trust anyone who was a friend to Castor Margin. "Have you seen Castor Margin lately?" I asked.

"Mayor Margin of Old Town? Of course I have. Do you know him?"

"We are old friends." I smiled "I could almost say we are related through marriage."

"How can that be?" DePratt looked genuinely puzzled. "I don't remember Margin ever leaving Redsky. He's lived here all his life and so has his wife. She was born here. I know her parents, the Oshinsky's, quite well."

"So do I. I used to be married to their daughter."

"As far as I know, Lane is their only daughter. She was married briefly before she married Castor. Her ex-husband was sent to a prison planet for murdering her brother Garth." He stared at me with sudden understanding. "Dan Griffin was his name. I remember now." His eyes searched my face. "You cannot be that man. It's impossible."

"It's him," Judge Wambaugh said. He must have been waiting to tell the news to the Prime Minister. "I handled his case. You took quite an interest in it, remember?"

Sir Charles DePratt was suddenly not a happy man. His face had taken on a pallid color. "I have a feeling I know why you are here," he murmured.

"I appealed to you for a new trial," I said, "but you denied me. Why?"

"I must have had good reasons. I don't remember. It's been ten years."

Strange, how selective his memory is. He remembers the case, even my name, but he doesn't remember the reason he denied my request. "Yes, it has. Some people spent those ten years under more enjoyable conditions than others." I picked up my glass of wine. "But I am not bitter. Maybe I should even be grateful. They've made me into what I am today, gave me a chance to travel, get to know new people."

I glanced at Meadow. She just shook her head. I could see the look of disapproval in her face. I grinned and emptied my glass.

"I think what the Major means is that he was commissioned by the Empire to do a job and he is going to do it, without being influenced by past occurrences," Meadow said into the uncomfortable silence.

I smiled at her, lifted my newly filled glass. "My lieutenant is correct. I am a citizen of the Empire, given considerable powers to deal with Redsky's problem, and I will deal with it in a proper manner, no matter what I have to do."

Meadow shook her head again. Her colorless eyes seemed to burn into mine. I didn't have her ability to read other people's emotions, but I could detect elevated pulses, increased breathing, over-productive sweat glands, and more.

Both, the Prime Minister and the judge were sweating profusely. Their wives and the other guests, even though they didn't really know what was going on, felt uneasy. Only Meadow looked cool and collected, as always, but I could guess what she was thinking. She knew me better than anyone did.

"No more wine," I told the serving girl, when she tried to refill my glass. "I think I've had enough." Turning to Lady Evana, who sat to my right, I said, "Forgive my rudeness, my Lady, but alcohol has the tendency to loosen my tongue."

She padded my hand and gave a strained laugh. "I believe most of us have that problem, Major Griffin. But I think I'll have another." Her hand lingered a little bit too long on mine and I registered her increased heartbeat. "Are you staying for the night? We have a guestroom."

I didn't need psychic abilities to read meaning into her words and I didn't have to look at Meadow to know what my answer had to be. "Thank you for the invitation, my Lady, but I have urgent business in Old Town, which can't wait. We'll have to get back tonight. Maybe another time."

I sensed her disappointment and heard her husband's suppressed sigh. "It is not safe to travel the roads at night," she said and smiled, her lips pulled into a little pout. "Maybe another time."

Chapter Seven

It was over three hundred kilometers from Capital City to Old Town. Our airsled was an older model, and we were lucky to reach 100 kilometers an hour. Our driver was the cautious type and never took us past the 90-kilometer mark. Since we had to drive through half a dozen small settlements and slow down at each one, it would take us nearly four hours to reach our destination.

It didn't matter. We were in no hurry. I would have liked to stay overnight with the Prime Minister, or to be more precise, with Lady Evana. I had sampled her passion and wouldn't have minded to dine some more, but I had no intentions to piss off Meadow even more.

Leaning back into my seat, I stared out of the window at the dark shadows flashing by. Hardly anyone traveled at night, because of the fierce night creatures, and lately because of roaming hostile native bands. Riding in a carriage pulled by horses was practically suicide, and even airsleds were deemed unsafe, the chance of one breaking down just too great.

Meadow had exchanged her sexy dress with a tight-fitting black uniform. A wide belt circled her tiny waist. From it hung a blaster as big as mine, and it wasn't there just for decoration. I thought she looked even sexier in this outfit. I wanted to tell her so, but before I could speak, she said, "You can be such an ass, Griffin!"

Oh-oh. When she used my last name, she was really pissed off. "If you say so." I didn't feel like arguing with her, but she had no mercy.

"I say so. When will you ever stop fucking every female who flutters her painted eyelids at you?"

I had to laugh at her outburst. "Jealous, Meadow?"

"My feelings have nothing to do with it. I worry about the mission. We can't afford to have it compromised by your actions."

"Aren't you forgetting something?"

"Like what?"

45

"I am your superior officer, Lieutenant."

"And I am you advisor and psych-officer. Don't you forget that, Major!"

Meadow, oh, Meadow. I reached for her hand. "And sometimes lover," I said softly.

A sound like a small explosion shifted our attention from each other. A shudder ran through our sled.

"We're going down!" the driver called out.

Going down maybe overstated it a little, because we floated never more than a meter above ground. The road ahead was plunged into sudden darkness as our headlights failed. Our sled dropped, began skipping across the uneven surface. We finally came to a halt as we crashed into an obstacle on the road.

"Stay inside and keep your head down," I told the driver. "Don't come out until one of us tells you so." Carefully opening my door, I dove out, rolled towards the edge of the road into the safety of the underbrush. My enhanced hearing told me that Meadow had made it to safety on the other side. It only took a moment for my eyes to adjust to night-vision and I had no problem seeing the object that stopped our sled.

A part of a huge tree trunk, neatly sliced on both ends. It had no business lying in the middle of the road. Somebody put it there.

Then I saw the vehicle about a hundred meters ahead of us, parked at the side of the road.

Sudden bright lights flooded the night, illuminating our sled. Two bulky figures, carrying rifles, stepped out of the other vehicle, started walking towards the airsled. I flattened myself into the high grass. This would be tricky. I knew these two weren't alone. There was at least one more person in that vehicle, possibly two.

I triggered the transmitter in the palate of my mouth and whispered, "Take care of the ones in the vehicle. Be careful."

"Understood," Meadow's answer came through the tiny speaker inside my ear.

I knew I could rely on her.

The pair reached the sled. Aiming their rifles, one of them called, "Come on out, and keep your hands up."

Even though I told the driver not to come out, he disobeyed my order. Slowly opening the door, he stuck out his head. "Don't shoot," he shouted. "I'm unarmed."

"Tell your passengers to throw out their guns."

46

"I'm alone." He stepped from the vehicle, hands in the air.

One of the two approached the sled carefully, while the other one covered him. "It's empty," he said after sticking his head into the interior of the sled.

"Impossible! They were seen leaving in this vehicle," said the other one. He turned to the driver. "Where are they?"

The driver shrugged. "I don't know."

The man smashed his rifle butt into the driver's belly, causing him to double over. "Does this jog your memory?"

The driver gasped for air and retched. "They left. I don't know where they are," he said between clenched teeth, pressing his hands into his belly.

Damn! I couldn't let them get away with this, but that bright light from the other vehicle pinned me into my hiding place. Where the hell was Meadow? What took her so long? I could just shoot these two, but would it be justified? Maybe they just wanted to talk to me.

Without warning, the one who had searched the sled pulled the trigger of his rifle, which he had so casually aimed at our driver. The sound of the exploding shell rang out sharply, echoed from the surrounding forest.

After that, things happened fast. The lights went out. My eyes adjusted automatically, but at first, I saw only two shadows. I was upon them before the images became clear pictures. One went down when I smashed the edge of my hand into his neck. Grabbing the one who shot the driver by the throat, I wrenched the rifle from his hands and lifted him into the air.

He kicked his dangling feet into my shins, but my high boots prevented him from doing any damage. His clawed fingers reached for my eyes. I threw him across the road, followed him with one jump and put my foot on his chest. Drawing my blaster, I pointed it at his head. "I think we need to talk," I said, keeping my voice at a normal level, but tempted to let the anger I felt rise to the surface.

I heard the one I sent into unconsciousness stirring, but I didn't even bother to look at him, I knew that Meadow already covered him with her weapon, as she came walking back towards us.

The man under my foot glared up at me. "Go to hell!" he cursed.

"The only one going to hell will be you, unless you decide to spill your guts," I told him coldly.

When my body and mind are in combat-mode, I am nothing but an emotionless and most efficient killing-machine. I'd have no trouble shooting him at the slightest provocation.

"Don't tell him anything," said the one on the ground behind me.

I heard a dull thud and a gasp. A booted foot into a ribcage will do that.

He cried out sharply, and then he cursed.

"The next one will hurt much more." Meadow's voice matched mine in its coldness.

"Bitch!" the man cursed, cried out again, much louder this time.

I increased the pressure of my booted foot, causing my man to utter a deep moan. "Easy," he groaned, "I think you broke some of my ribs."

"Good," I said. "Pain can help a man to make up his mind so much faster."

"Alright. What do you want to know?"

"Who hired you?"

"Nobody. We just wanted to rob you."

He screamed when I shifted my weight. "Who?" I asked.

"I don't know."

"Shut up!" his friend told him. A dull thud caused him to be silent.

Taking my foot off the man's chest, I bent, pulled him into a standing position. He didn't look too good. One of his arms hung uselessly down his side and his face was gray. But I had no mercy with him. He signed his own death warrant when he killed our driver. "Talk now and I'll kill you quickly. I promise it will be painless."

"And if I don't talk?"

I gave his collar a twist. "You'll suffer, I promise that also."

He was dying, but he didn't know it, yet. He couldn't stand by himself. My throw had broken his back.

"I told you, I don't know," he said with a weak voice. "We never know when we do a job. It's better that way."

"You kill people for hire?"

He nodded. "It's nothing personal. Just business." He grimaced. "We're independent contractors."

"Just business. Yeah. I take it quite personal when somebody wants to kill me." I let go of him. He collapsed, lay on the ground, whimpering. Even though he didn't deserve a quick death, I shot him between the eyes with a short burst of my laser. Turning, I looked at Meadow. The man she was guarding lay motionless in front of her.

"Kill him?" she asked.

I shook my head and looked at the vehicle at the side of the road. "How many?"

"There were two."

"Dead?"

She nodded. Meadow had no compunction killing anyone. Beautiful, sexy, deadly. That was Meadow.

I bent to examine our driver, but as I already knew, he was dead. Checking out the sled confirmed my suspicion. Someone had tampered with it. A micro-bomb destroyed enough of the drive to render it useless. "We'll take their vehicle," I told Meadow.

She gave the man on the ground a kick between the ribs. He opened his eyes. "Can you operate that airsled of yours?" she asked.

He opened his mouth to say something, probably something nasty, but one look into her cold eyes and another at his dead companion changed his mind and he just nodded.

"Alright, let's get going." Meadow watched him rise to his feet.

"Bring that man," I told him, pointing at the still body of our driver.

"What about my brother?" he asked.

"He's of no use to us," Meadow said cruelly. "We'll leave him for the vultures."

"But he's my brother!"

She shrugged. "He's dead. You can pick him up later, or what's left of him. Now, move!"

He stumbled towards the airsled, pulling the driver with him. He cursed when he saw his two dead companions slumped in their seats. "Get rid of them!" Meadow commanded. He obeyed, pulled them out of the sled and dragged them into the shrubbery. With a look at our dead driver, "What should I do with him?"

"Into the trunk," I said.

He opened up the trunk. It was full of tools and other stuff. "Throw it out," I told him.

He grunted, but did as told. With the dead driver in the trunk, we were ready to move on.

Meadow made herself comfortable in the backseat. I joined our new driver in the front. "Take us to Old Town," I said. "And don't try to be a hero!"

* * * *

Desk Sergeant Kriemer didn't look pleased when we interrupted his little snooze in his comfortable chair behind his big desk.

"It's three o'clock and the middle of the night," he complained. "Couldn't you have waited until morning?"

I gave him a hard look and flipped open my cape to let him see the insignia on my shirt. I was in no mood to play any courtesy games.

"S...so...sorry, sir." Stumbling over the words, he rose from his chair and gave our prisoner a second look. "He doesn't look familiar."

"I'm charging him with the murder of one Josef Sideman, our driver. Book him and throw him in Jail. First thing tomorrow morning, I want you to find out who he is and whom he runs with. Understand?"

"Yes, sir!" He almost snapped to attention. I was beginning to like this man. Before we walked out of the door, I turned and said, "Please, tell Sergeant Mitas I want to see him in the morning. He knows where to find me. Not too early, though. I need to catch up on my sleep."

Outside, Meadow smiled at me. "You're sure you want to spend all that time sleeping?"

I grinned at her. "I wanted to tell you before that you look absolutely sexy in your tight-fitting uniform," I said. "I don't think it would take much persuasion to keep me up a little longer."

She laughed and hooked her arm into mine. "It never does," she said.

How well she knew me. I felt glad her anger at me had dissipated. But then again, she was most passionate when angry.

* * * *

I didn't get much rest that night, and not just because of Meadow. My communicator behind my ear sprang to life at exactly 7:00 a.m.

"Major?" The ghostlike voice sounded clear and brisk.

"Acknowledged. What is it, Killic?"

"I hope I didn't wake you, Major."

"As a matter of fact, you have. This better be good."

Beside me, Meadow turned around. Yawning, she watched me out of sleepy eyes.

"It's neither good nor bad," Killic said, "but I think you should come back to base. There are some developments."

"Give me a couple of hours. Unless it can't wait."

"It's not that urgent. We just thought you'd want to know." He broke the connection.

"Problems?" Meadow asked, sitting up. I looked at her exposed breasts and I felt a sudden pounding in my loins.

Damn that Killic! Whatever it was, I felt certain it could wait, but just knowing some important information may have come up, I couldn't ignore it. "Killic thinks we should return to base."

"Both of us?" she asked, pulling the covers over her head.

"Both of us," I said and, with a regretful look at the outlines of her body beneath the thin covers, I got up.

When I came out of the shower, Meadow stood naked in front of the large mirror, studying her slim body with a critical eye. Striking a pose, she pushed out her round, smooth buttocks. Her eyes met mine in the mirror.

Why the hell did she have to do that?

"You'll never change," I said.

"What?" she asked, giving me an innocent look.

"You were a teasing bitch when you joined my team, and you still are."

She padded across the cold stone floor, stood in front of me, her pale eyes staring into mine. "Isn't that what attracts you to me?" she asked with a purring voice and turned to walk away.

I slapped one of her wiggling cheeks. "You know me so well, don't you?"

Any other time I would have taken her up on her teasing invitation, but I knew this was not the time. With a coded impulse, I suppressed the desire to grab her and throw her onto the bed, making my body immune to any external stimulation.

An hour later, we took our skimmer up and headed for the spaceport. It only took thirty minutes to reach our destination.

While the rest of Redsky was classified a Class D planet, the spaceport had no such restrictions. Surrounded by a five-meter high electric fence, it kept intruders out, but it also kept anyone from leaving without permission.

Robotic sentries guarded the airspace above. Uninvited guests were simply shot down. The area inside the fence was considered property of Imperial Terra. Redsky's laws did not apply here.

After receiving clearance from the tower, the spaceport computer took control of our skimmer and set us down automatically in a designated space.

I looked across the tarmac, empty, except for our small battle cruiser, which squatted like an ugly black bug beside the hangar, ready to pounce on anyone who might irritate it. Visitors from other systems did not drop in on a regular basis. Only freighters and trade-ships came to visit every few months. They never stayed very long.

Meadow and I walked across the polished terrace towards the Administration building, a huge glass-covered complex that housed not only the living quarters of the clerks and guards, but also laboratories, guest rooms, and storage facilities, even a jail. I knew it quite well. I spent some time in it ten years ago, before they shipped me to one of the Empire's prison planets.

The guard by the entrance stood there merely for appearance sake, in reality he was nothing more than an armed doorman. No hostiles would ever get this far. He saluted smartly when we approached and opened the door for us.

We found it cool and refreshing inside. The building had climate control and all the amenities of civilized life, but it didn't really mean that much to Meadow and me. Neither of us grew up in decadent luxuries. We were more comfortable and at home in rougher, more primitive surroundings. Then again...it was nice to be pampered once in awhile.

Killic waited for us in one of the rooms we claimed for our base while we stayed on Redsky. A skinny little man stood beside him, stroking his black goatee.

Professor Goldblat.

"Ahh, Major Griffin," the Professor beamed. I could guess why. He must have finished his pet project. "Dida is anxiously waiting for your first report."

He was referring to D.I.D.A., which stood for Digital Intelligence Data Analyzer, Professor Goldblat's brainchild. This was the first one, a prototype.

"I can hardly wait to be hooked up to it," I said, maybe a little bit too sarcastically.

"Not *hooked-up to it*," the professor corrected me. "*Joined to her*. It will be like making love to a beautiful woman. By the way, you'll be the first one."

Beside him, Killic smirked, his blue eyes twinkling in his tanned face. Big and bulky, he looked like a giant beside the professor. I waited for him to make a remark, but he kept his mouth shut. So did Meadow, which surprised me.

"And you, Lieutenant Rainseeker?" Professor Goldblat addressed Meadow. He never used anyone's first name. "Have you been taking good care of your Major and kept him out of trouble?"

She smiled. "Keeping him out of trouble is nearly an impossible task. I think trouble searches him out."

"So I've heard. There was an attempt on your life?" He looked at me.

"It seems that way." I nodded. "We've dealt with it."

"I know that, too." His black eyes stared at me from under bushy eyebrows. "Even though you've been given unlimited powers, I suggest you use them discretely, Major Griffin. Remember, this is a Class D planet. You should limit the use of atomic weapons."

"What use are superior weapons when we're not allowed to use them?" I asked.

"You can use them, but only as a last resort. Consider our enemy and why we are here. We don't want to draw unnecessary attention to you and your abilities." He smiled and padded me on the shoulder, the way a father would his son. In a sense, he was partially my father. He had created all the tiny devices I carried inside my body. "I think it's time for you to meet Dida."

Chapter Eight

The D.I.D.A. didn't look too impressive. A one-meter square shiny cube with a bunch of blinking lights and connection ports in the front panel, it sat on top of a sturdy metal frame.

"Make yourself comfortable," Professor Goldblat pointed to a black chair with an adjustable transparent half-globe on top of it. After I followed his invitation, he said, "I'll leave you now. My lab-assistant will hook you up. I'll be next door in the observation room. He opened the door to let in a young woman in a white lab coat.

"I am Licia," she said, giving me a little smile. "This won't hurt a bit. So I'm told." She approached my chair. "Please, sit straight. I'm going to position the transfer module over your skull."

As soon as she pulled the transparent half-globe over my eyes, everything went black for a second, and then the lights came back on. Disoriented and slightly dizzy for a moment, I realized I wasn't sitting in my chair anymore, instead I found myself standing in a sea of yellow flowers. The sky above me seemed alive with changing colors. They moved like the northern lights on a cold, clear winter's night on good old Earth. I'd only seen it once, but the beauty of that sight had enthralled me.

"Does this make you happy?"

I turned around slowly to look at the speaker.

She stood not far from me, her flowing robe and loose hair fluttered in the warm breeze that I hadn't been aware of before.

"Did I get it right?" she asked with a soft melodious voice.

"What?"

"The colors?" She pointed at the moving lights in the sky. "I created them from your memory."

"I don't understand?"

She laughed. "Forgive me. I thought this would put you at ease."

"Where am I?" I asked, but I already knew.

"You are inside me. At least your mind is." She came closer. I could see the outlines of her body beneath the semi-transparent material of her robe.

"What should I call you?" I asked.

"My designation is D.I.D.A., but you can call me anything you like."

"I will call you *Angel*."

"Why?"

I shrugged. "Because you look like one."

"Alright." Laughing again, she let the robe slip from her shoulders. It floated in slow motion gently to the ground, covering the flowers.

There wasn't a blemish on her perfectly formed body.

She reached out with a slim arm and touched my cheek with one finger. Her touch sent gentle shockwaves through my whole body. Only now, I became aware of my own nakedness, and my body reacted to her touch.

Sinking to her knees, she stretched out among the flowers and held out her arms. I fell between her opening thighs, and crushed my chest against her soft breasts. Her kisses tasted like sweet berries and her skin felt like smooth silk against mine. She stroked my back with tender hands, let her fingers trail down past my hips, and caressed the crease between my clenching buttocks. Her long fingernails dragged gently across my skin, making me shiver with delight.

I began to move my pelvis between her spread thighs, searching for an opening into her luscious body. Something warm and wet grabbed the tip of my probing organ, sucked it gently into an incredible softness, and I thought I would die right there. No woman had ever felt like this.

"This is my first complete joining since I became aware," she whispered and moved against me.

She gave me constant pleasure, an orgasm that went on and on. How long it lasted, I don't know. Time meant nothing. I floated in a sea of colors and pleasure. There seemed to be music, but I couldn't be sure.

Entering a state of tranquility I've never attained before, I felt at peace with the universe and myself. Everything was as it should be.

The gentle murmur I heard became more urgent, more insistent. Then I heard the voice of a woman.

"Major Griffin, are you alright?"

Opening my eyes, I saw a woman's anxious face above me. Licia, the assistant. "Are you alright?" she asked again.

I looked down at myself, expecting to be naked, but I wasn't.

"How are you feeling?" She pressed something cool against my neck.

"I feel fine," I said, taking a deep breath. "I don't think I've ever felt like this before. My mind is clear and it seems I've slept for days."

Licia smiled, and then studied the instrument she was holding. "The readings confirm that you are fine."

I stared at the shiny cube in front of me. "How long was I connected to that thing?"

"About fifteen minutes."

"You're sure?"

"I'm sure. I was the one who hooked you up, remember?"

I rose, still staring at the blinking lights. I recognized a pattern, a code. *Take care, Daniel Griffin. Until next time. Angel.*

"I need to talk to Professor Goldblat." I said.

I found him in a room next door, bent over a screen on his desk, studying it intently. "She likes you," he said when I walked in.

"What the hell is that thing?" I was angry with him. Why, I didn't know.

"Dida is not a *thing*, Griffin. She has a personality and is actually quite sensitive. You'll hurt her feelings by calling her a *thing*."

"Are you telling me that box is a sentient being?"

He looked up from his screen. "That box is the body of the most sophisticated artificial intelligence ever created by man. More powerful and intelligent than even the Central Computer on Earth."

A series of beeps made him look at the screen in front of him. Frowning, he stared at it for a moment, and then he smiled. Beckoning me to come closer, he said, "I think this is meant for you."

I looked at a message on the screen: *Don't be so shallow, Daniel. The shape of a body means nothing. It's what inside that counts.*

"Can it…can she hear us?"

He nodded. "Every word. Right now we only communicate through writing, but I'll hook her up to a speaker to give her a voice." He pulled on his goatee. "Dida provided me with a report of the physical examination she gave you and also an evaluation of your mental state. You're in excellent physical condition and mentally you are stable. She has a couple of slight concerns: Your thoughts of revenge and your obsession with sex. Both are hidden quite well and under control, but they are present. Guard yourself against them."

"My obsession with sex?" I had to laugh. "Tell me, Professor, did you program my…how should I put it…my *joining* with Dida?"

"You don't program Dida. She has her own mind and complete free will. She uses whatever means she thinks appropriate to extract information. I named her Digital Intelligence Data Analyzer, because initially, that's what she was supposed to be, but she turned out to be so much more. Her intellect is far superior to anything in existence. I am quite proud of her."

"Children have a habit of disappointing their parents," I said, cautioning him.

"So they do," he said and looked at me, smiling fondly. "But I have faith in my children."

"Did she tell you what happened when I was connected to her?" I asked.

"No."

"You don't want to know?"

"It doesn't really matter. What matters to me is the information she gathers and the conclusions she draws from it. Did she hurt you? No? Good. She never will. That is the only restriction I programmed into her. She can never do or initiate anything that will cause harm to a human. Ever. Even if it means her own destruction. She will make recommendations, that's all."

"Self-preservation is a strong motivator in any living being," I said.

"Usually." He nodded in agreement. "But not always." Bending over his computer screen, he said, "But now you must excuse me, Major, Dida promised to help me in another small project of mine. I believe Sergeant Killic wants to talk with you."

Killic was anxiously waiting for me. So were Cherryh, Kelsey, and Wu, the remaining three members of my team.

"We heard about your little encounter," Cherryh said.

I smiled grimly. "News travels fast, even on Redsky."

"The Chief of Police himself contacted us. He was not happy. Apparently, the man you brought in claims that you murdered his brother in cold blood, after they approached you to offer their help when your sled broke down. He's filing a formal complaint."

That really made me laugh. "I didn't really expect anything else from Chief Slovinsky. He's an old acquaintance. I should have shot the prisoner, just to save myself some aggravation. I guess we'll never find out who he worked for."

"On a more positive note," Killic broke in, "the *Eagles* have been released and we've had our first reports."

He referred to the surveillance satellites our technicians put into orbit.

"We've detected activity in the southwestern part of the Strathon Mountains. Two small spacecraft of unknown origin landed and took off again."

"It confirms earlier reports," I said.

"Those reports were only vague. Now we have pinpointed the exact location," Cherry said.

Wu produced a map of Newland and Dangar, the province to the north. Somebody had drawn a red circle around an area at the edge of the desert in Dangar, the same location Commander Ryker had shown me on his map.

"I had planned to pay this place a visit in the near future," I said, "but this adds some urgency to my plans. I have a few things to take care off in Old Town, and then Meadow and I will get on our way. We'll discuss the details after I've taken a long, hot bath."

Chapter Nine

Stanislaus Slovinsky had never been on the list of my closest friends. In fact, I've always hated his guts. Especially since he and Castor Margin had been bosom-buddies.

Now Castor was the mayor of Old Town and Stanislaus the Chief of Police.

And I the Negotiator from Terra, a man hated by both men.

Strange, how Lady Fate sometimes plays her cards.

"I had to release the man. We have only your word against his, Dan."

"It's Major Griffin, if you don't mind," I said coldly. He used to call me *Daniella*, until the day I broke his nose. It never did heal right and he never forgave me for it.

He leaned forward, his pudgy face taking on the color of the sky outside. "Alright, you want to play hardball. You always did. You don't impress me with your fancy black outfit, your big laser gun and your badge. As far as I'm concerned, you're still Dan Griffin, a hoodlum we sent to a prison colony. I'm warning you. Even you won't get away with murder. We have our own justice here and we take care of our own."

"Like you did ten years ago?"

Half rising in his chair, he pointed an accusing finger at me. "You've been warned, Griffin! Do your job, only your job. Do not stick your nose where it doesn't belong!"

"Are you afraid of what I might find?"

"You will find nothing! Dammit, why can't you just leave things alone? Why the hell did you have to come back?"

"I didn't come by choice, Chief Slovinsky. You know, there is one thing that piques my curiosity. Everyone I talk to seems to have a problem with my presence here. I'm telling you the same thing I told Castor Margin. I will not go out of my way to stir up trouble, but I will pursue any lead I come across in my investigation."

"What investigation?"

I smiled. "You don't have clearance to receive that kind of information, sorry."

"Why do military people always have to be so secretive? Do they think the rest of the population is a bunch of morons?" He gave me a calculating look. "You are naïve if you believe that you can keep your real reason for coming here a secret. We know about the Stardogs."

I kept my face neutral, trying to hide my surprise. "Somebody's been talking out of school."

"I am the police chief. I have access to information." He stared at me with a triumphant smirk. "So go and find your Stardogs and then get the hell off my planet, *Major* Griffin of the Mighty Empire."

"I'll leave when *I* decide, Chief Slovinsky." I tipped the edge of my helmet and turned to leave.

Before I was out of the door, he called after me, "And don't forget to pay Olson Rentals for the airsled you wrecked!"

Shaking my head, I closed the door behind me. He had been an idiot then and he was one still. How he ever made Chief of Police was beyond me. However, I remembered his parents. His father a councilman, his mother chief-surgeon at the only hospital in Old Town. People of great influence and with connections.

There had been rumors that his father was a member of *The Winged Serpent*, a criminal organization, involved in slavery and gunrunning, but those had only been rumors.

Outside Slovinsky's office, a uniformed officer approached me. I recognized him as one of the two I had encountered in *Triton's Tavern*. "Keep walking," he said in a low voice, "and don't look at me."

"What do you want?"

"Darl Mitas is a friend of mine. I hear you're one of his. Some friendly advice, watch your back. Don't trust anyone. They want you dead."

He was gone before I could comment. It would have been nice to know who "they" were.

Outside, the sun was shining. A few white clouds in the reddish sky promised rain. I remembered days like this when I had taken Lane to watch the illegal dogfights. The dogs were most vicious just before the rain. The low pressure did something to their brains.

Sighing, I headed for the parking lot where I left the airsled. I saw the two men in long black coats before they started walking towards me, registered the slight bulge on their right hip where they carried their guns.

"Dan Griffin?" the older one of them said, coming closer, while the younger one hung back.

"You know who I am," I said, watching his hands. They'd never even clear their holsters before my gun would be in my hand, but I didn't think they'd be stupid enough to try to gun me down in broad daylight.

I waited until he stood in front of me. "Careful," I warned him when he pulled back one side of his coat to reveal his weapon.

"I'm not going to shoot you," he said and smiled. He looked like a cave-viper just before she struck. "Just wanted to identify myself."

Looking at his sidearm, I said, "I could arrest you right here for violation of Paragraph Seventeen, Article Twelve, Section Fifteen from the Imperial Law Book of Rules and Regulations regarding the different classes of occupied and unoccupied planets."

"I am quite aware of those rules, Major Griffin. I have clearance for this weapon, just like you. I am Inspector McClaren of Spaceport Internal Security, and my partner is Sergeant Marc Cleaver."

"I doubt your clearance allows you to carry such a weapon outside of the spaceport."

He shrugged. "Sometimes we have to bend regulations a bit. The Empire is far from here. Those eggheads who write the rules have never set foot on an alien, hostile planet." He grinned. "You yourself, you've bent the rules ever since you shot those renegades in the desert."

"So I did. What is it you want, Inspector McClaren?"

"Nothing, really. You know, I've been on this forsaken planet twelve years now." When my eyebrows lifted, he nodded. "Yes, I was there when they brought you in chains ten years ago. I was just a rookie then. You may not remember me, but I remember you. They took you away as a criminal. Now...here you are, back, a free man. A representative of the Mighty Empire. Isn't it a good feeling to be above the law? To have the power to do whatever you wish?"

"What exactly is your point, Inspector?" I was getting impatient. Whatever he planned, I knew, it couldn't be anything good.

"I don't know how much you get paid, probably a lot more than I get. Maybe not." He smiled. "Anyway, I feel underpaid. I think my job entitles me to more than I receive. Most of us think that way, but not many do anything about it. I am one of the few who did. I know, we're supposed to keep contact with the locals to a minimum, but I believe in having friends and I've made some. But you know how it is." He spread his hands. "Friends expect certain favors from you…if you're in a position to give them."

"A real friend expects nothing," I said. "I still don't understand what you're trying to tell me."

He sighed. "What I'm trying to say…if in your investigation my name somehow pops up, I hope you will close one eye and won't look too closely. A favor from one professional to another. I'm sure you understand."

I studied him with open receptors. His heartbeat was elevated and beads of perspiration covered his forehead. A nervous tick made his left eyelid tremble slightly. His jovial manner was just a cover to hide his fear. This man was deep into something he shouldn't be messing with and he feared discovery. Suddenly, he looked like a cornered rat.

Cornered rats are dangerous.

"I don't know whom you're involved with or what, and at this point I don't want to know," I said softly, "but I suggest you take stock of whatever it is and make sure you're friends are worth your loyalty." I gave him a little smile. "Just some friendly advice from one professional to another. Now, if you'll excuse me, Inspector McClaren, I'm on a tight schedule. "I winked. "Have to earn my pay, you know."

Grinning crookedly, he stepped aside. "Nice to talk to you, Major Griffin," he said as I walked by him. "Maybe you and I can have a drink together, sometime."

"Maybe," I said.

"I might be of some help to you," he called after me. "I'm sure you could use another friend. I know you don't have too many."

"You're right, I don't," I murmured to myself.

My driver, Anton, looked at me anxiously when he opened the door for me. "Everything alright?" he asked.

I nodded.

"That was Inspector McClaren of Spaceport Security," he said.

"You know him?"

"Sort of." He hesitated. "My father told me not to trust him and to stay away from him. He's bad news."

"I should talk to your father. Maybe he can tell me a little more about our inspector."

Anton shook his head. "I'm afraid that's not possible. My father was killed last month in a skirmish with the natives. He was a sergeant at the Garrison."

"I'm sorry to hear that."

He pulled out a handkerchief and blew his nose noisily, and then he looked at me with a little smile. "It's the dust, you know. I suffer from allergies."

"They must have medicine for that," I said.

"They do, but unless you're in Essential Services, you don't qualify. Lots of stuff is rationed, you know. Now that my father is dead, I don't qualify anymore. They'll ship me back to Earth with the next transport. I'm considered *useless baggage*." He laughed. "Did you know that I was born here? This is my home. I don't know anything else."

"How about your mother?"

"Kidnapped by slave traders, probably." He shrugged. "Nobody knows for sure. She and a friend went visiting someone in Old Town. She never came back. I was ten."

Damn it! I felt sorry for the kid. He looked older than he was. One of the lab technicians recommended him when I asked for someone who knew how to operate an airsled. It wasn't that I couldn't have done it myself, but I wanted some time to think undisturbed and, frankly, I needed the company.

"Maybe I can put in a good word for you," I said.

His face brightened. "Do you think you could?"

"I'll try, son, but now let's get back home."

Chapter Ten

None of the moons had come up yet, and in the darkness, the large skimmer settled softly onto the ground inside a small grove of tall trees. The skimmer was part of the equipment we brought with us to Redsky, nothing like the airsleds the people here were used to seeing, but the chance of anyone spying it against the sky had been very slim. This area was sparsely populated and the closest town, Rockwald, about twenty kilometers away.

We left Old Town in the late afternoon, and it took us just a little over six hours to fly the 700 kilometers north. The caravan we were going to join should be coming through *Tangai* within a week, plenty of time for us to get there.

I turned towards Darl Mitas, who had operated the skimmer. "Let's hope the old man Ben Dar is still alive and welcomes us."

Darl grinned. "Well, the only way to find out is to go and see."

He unbuckled and stepped outside.

Meadow opened her eyes lazily. "Guess it's time." She touched my hand. "Be careful, Dan."

"Don't worry, we'll be back in no time. We're only visiting an old friend."

I looked at Niels DePratt, the fourth member of our party. He hadn't said much during the trip, guessing that his presence didn't please any of us. He was with us only because Commander Ryker insisted he come along. As military observer. Orders from above.

More likely spy or watchdog. It was too obvious. Especially since he was the son of the Prime Minister.

He grimaced when I looked at him. "Go ahead," he said, "I'll just hang around here with your lady friend. I won't be lonely."

"She is not my lady friend. She's a lieutenant with the Terran Interplanetary Space Force," I said.

"Ah, a fellow officer."

"You may be a lieutenant, DePratt, but you're not in the same league as Lieutenant Rainseeker. She outranks you by a light year." I didn't like him and I didn't like his whole attitude. He spelled trouble. I made no effort to hide my dislike for him.

Meadow just smiled, pursing her lips.

I followed Darl, who was already walking towards the house that lay somewhere ahead. The place seemed quiet, nothing unexpected this close to midnight. They were probably all asleep by now.

I banged against the heavy wooden door, and after awhile we heard footsteps on the other side.

"Who wants in?" a harsh voice called out.

"It's Dan Griffin. I came to see Ben Dar."

After a moment of silence, another voice answered. "Ben Dar is dead. Go away." It was the voice of a girl.

"Is that Aleethy, Ben Dar's beautiful little daughter?" I asked, after the initial shock of knowing that the old man was dead had worn off.

"Yes, this is Aleethy," the girl's voice answered, "but you're not Dan Griffin. He's dead, too. My father told me so."

"I'm alive, little *tika*. Open up and see for yourself." I had called her *little flower-worm*, a name only I used to call her.

I heard a suppressed cry, and then the grating sound of a heavy timber being pushed aside. The door swung open and I looked at the tall, slim figure standing in the doorway. She gasped and flung herself into my arms. "Dan, Dan," she sobbed, clinging to me. "It is really you. Oh, I'm so happy to see you."

Gently, I disengaged myself and looked at her. Even in the flickering light of the lantern, I could see she had grown into a beautiful young woman. "I'm happy to see you, too, little *tika*," I said and laughed. "Not so little anymore. Last time I saw you, you were a skinny pest, all eyes and teeth, but look at you now!"

My eyes rested on the swell of her breasts, one of them half revealed inside her loose-fitting robe. She colored slightly, giggled and pulled me into the house. Entering, I saw the man standing in the shadows of the hallway. He held a large pistol in his hand. I recognized it as the one I gave the old man Ben Dar many years ago.

The man was short and slightly overweight, past middle age. I didn't know him.

He scowled, staring at me.

"Relax, Vardal." Aleethy told him. "This is an old friend of my father's." She turned to me and smiled, "and of mine."

"How about me?" Darl's voice came from the door. "Am I welcome, too?" He stepped into the hallway and closed the door behind him.

"I'm sorry," the girl apologized. "You look familiar, but I don't remember you."

"That's Darl Mitas, a good friend of mine. He knew your father," I said.

She smiled at him. "Then you're welcome."

It was Darl's turn to become flustered, and I couldn't blame him. I had to stare at Aleethy, not quite believing this was the same awkward little girl I used to tease and play childish games with just a little over a decade ago.

Noticing my eyes, she lowered her dark lashes and pulled the robe closer around her tiny waist, which only accentuated her hips and ample bosom. She turned and walked into the kitchen, and I admired the play of her rounded buttocks beneath the thin material of her robe.

Darl exhaled sharply beside me. "A jewel among jewels," he muttered under his breath, and I had to agree. She certainly was.

She lit another oil lamp and invited us to sit down. "My father's been dead for five years," she answered an unspoken question, "and my mother left soon after he died...with a merchant from Dangar. I haven't seen her since."

It didn't surprise me. Her mother, much younger than Ben Dar and very pretty, had not been against going to bed with other men.

I should know!

We talked for a time until I felt certain I could trust her and the man Vardal, her business manager and in charge of her ranch. Ben Dar had been raising the finest riding animals in the area, and when he died, Aleethy kept the business going.

She was not only beautiful, but also quite smart, as I soon discovered.

"We need a place where we can hide our airsled," I told her, "and we want to purchase four of your beasts."

"Anything you need, Dan," she said, brushing a strand of black hair out of her face. "Are you staying for awhile?"

"A couple of days, but then we must move on to Tangai, where we will join the caravan."

Maybe it was only my imagination or just wishful thinking, but I'm certain I saw the promise of pleasant moments in her dark eyes, when she looked at me over the rim of her mug, while sipping a hot drink.

I felt uneasy and guilty, remembering Meadow, who would know as soon as she laid eyes on Aleethy. Damn her gift anyway, and besides...I wasn't married to her.

I sent Darl to get her and DePratt. My assumption had, of course, been correct. Meadow stalked into the room, angrier than a *horned tree-cat*, and even behind the contact lenses, which hid her alien eyes, I could see the burning fire. The glare she shot at me could have killed a *Gar.*

"Well, well," she said sweetly. "You finally remembered us. I'm surprised you thought of us at all."

"This is Aleethy," I said lamely. "She's an old friend. And this is Meadow...a new friend."

Meadow stared at the girl. "I'm sure she is friendly, but not old."

As I said, Aleethy wasn't stupid, and she returned Meadow's icy stare. "That's true," she said in a matching voice. "Which can't be said about you." She looked at me. "I'm surprised you call her your friend. I thought you'd be choosier."

Women! Curse them all!

I would never understand them.

* * * *

Aleethy invited me to sleep in one of the spare bedrooms in the main house, while the others had to sleep in the bunkhouse with the ranch hands. I accompanied Darl back to the skimmer to get a couple of things I wanted to give to Aleethy. We put the skimmer into one of the large outbuildings to hide it, away from prying eyes. Then I went back into the house and headed for my room.

My defense-system automatically scanned the room as I entered.

Somebody was in the bedroom.

I detected the soft breathing of a woman. My memory web revealed the identity of the intruder.

I opened the door and looked at her lovely naked form sprawled on the bed.

She smiled. "Hi, Dan, I thought we should celebrate your homecoming."

Two long steps took me to the bed and then we lay in each other's arms. "Aleethy," I moaned. "I can't believe how beautiful you've become."

She laughed and began undressing me. When she touched me, I

reacted immediately and rolled between her opening thighs. My hard organ searched for her pussy, but she held me back. "Don't hurry, love. We have all night. Even though I can't wait to feel you inside me, I want to enjoy the anticipation of that moment for as long as possible."

When she finally opened herself to me, the pleasure seemed almost unbearable and her cry of joy joined my own harsh shout. I fought for control and managed to keep a slow and steady rhythm, bringing her to a climax several times.

I remembered her mother, a wild, passionate woman. Aleethy was a lot like her, but her passion ran much deeper, more honest.

We made love for over an hour. She finally cried out for me to stop. When I came, she held me close, her body still until I finished. Then she kissed me deeply and lay back, a satisfied smile on her lips.

"I love celebrations," she said dreamily and closed her eyes.

* * * *

I woke to find her covering my chest with kisses.

"Why don't we celebrate some more." She smiled and rolled on top of me. As the warm walls of her pussy closed around my stiff mast, I chuckled. "Who am I to argue, little tika."

Smiling, she slowly rotated her hips. Her long black hair fell across my chest, tickling my skin like a blanket of soft feathers. I studied her lovely face and her dark eyes, as they stared into mine, remembering the big-eyed, shy little girl who used to sit in my lap, combing my hair.

Her smile faded and she sobbed as the first wave of a tremendous orgasm gripped her body, and soon she bucked uncontrollably above me. When she sagged against me, she whispered, "Oh, Dan, I don't know if I can ever stop. You feel so good inside me."

I laughed and held her steady as she began bucking again, whishing the time with her would never end. It was already getting light outside, when she climbed out of bed to go to the bathroom.

"I am famished," Aleethy said, as she combed her long hair. She looked at herself in the mirror of the dresser. He eyes met mine. "You look hungry, too." She laughed. "But somehow I don't think it is food you want." She turned around and touched my hand. "It's been wonderful, Dan. You are wonderful and I wish we could be lovers. Real lovers, I mean."

I bent to kiss her inviting lips and her arms went around my neck. "My little tika," I murmured into her fragrant hair, "you are so beautiful, and it wouldn't take much to fall in love with you. We could be lovers, but it wouldn't be fair to you. I am not the same *happy-go-lucky daredevil* you knew."

"I know, love, I know," she said, swallowing back a sob. "I sensed it last night when you walked through my door. There is something inside you that scares the hell out of me. Something cold and distant. It prevents you from ever really loving anybody."

I pulled her up, held her tight and wiped her wet cheeks.

She smiled up at me. "Do you know that I had a crush on you from the first time you rode in with my dad? But you always thought I was such a pest."

I had to laugh, remembering. "We became pretty good friends later. You always told me you loved me…like a brother."

"I did. That was the only way you let me sit in your lap." She giggled. "I guess it was silly of a ten year old to want to be taken seriously by a young man twice her age." She lowered her dark lashes. "When I was thirteen, I used to fantasize how we would play hide and seek and how you would suddenly rip off my panties and ravish me."

She blushed as she told me this and I laughed. "I never would have guessed. Maybe if I would have known…"

"You never would have, Dan." She was suddenly serious. "You only had eyes for my mother. Not that I blame you. She came on to everybody else. Did you ever sleep with her?"

That question made me uncomfortable. "Let us not talk about your mother." I kissed her lightly. "Tell me more about your sex-fantasies."

She sighed, her shoulders slumping. "So you did sleep with her, the slut. Am I as good as she?"

I took her sweet face between my hands. "Aleethy, let the past lie," I said gently. "Your mother was what she was, she couldn't help herself."

Her dark eyes bored into mine. "You didn't answer my question, Dan. Am I as good as she?"

"You are cream, my little tika. So lovely, so beautiful. Lucky is the man who is chosen by you." I held her tightly as she cried on my shoulder.

"I haven't had much experience with men, Dan," she said between sobs. "You are the third one. The first one was a boy from a neighboring ranch. We only did it a few times, until I found out he did it with his younger sister and her girlfriend, too. The other one was a merchant I had deals with."

I chuckled. "You don't have to tell me all this."

"I know, but I'm afraid, Dan. I love sex. I really enjoyed doing it with you, and with the others. But I don't want to turn out like my mother."

"You have to do what ever makes you happy, Aleethy. Nobody else can help you there."

She wiped her tears away and smiled bravely. "You are so strong, Dan. Too bad, things are the way they are. I think I could be happy with you." She looked down at my erection and giggled. "Very happy."

I lifted her up. Her legs went around my hips, and with a deep sigh, she let her pussy slide over my stiff member. Her lovely round buttocks quivered in my hands, as she moved them back and forth.

In the mirror, I could see her beautiful naked body writhe against mine, and it made me swell even more inside her.

"Oh, Dan," she moaned against my ear, "what are you doing to me?"

"Making love," I said, watching her buttocks in the mirror. "Making sweet, sweet love."

Afterward, we lay together on the bed. I cuddled her in my arms, stroking her silky, black hair, her smooth naked back, and her round buttocks.

Chapter Eleven

We left two days later. The riding animals we purchased from Aleethy were big and strong scaly beasts. *Harsa*, bred for the harsh country we were about to enter. It took us six hours to reach the outskirts of Tangai. The town hadn't changed much since I'd been there last. Spreading along the south side of the river Tan, it was close to the border of Dangar, the country to the north. Dangar was a long narrow stretch of mostly desert, framed by high, rugged mountains, the only passable connection to the north countries, and travelers took the long trek only with a caravan.

We'd planned to search out one of these caravans and to travel with it until we reached our destination. The alien base was reported to be south of the Strathon Mountains, a narrow ridge, which ran eastward, cutting Dangar almost in half.

The aroma of grilled *Gandor* tantalized our noses, and we decided to stop in one of the taverns, possibly even take a room until we could locate a caravan.

There were no New-Wave settlers in Tangai, only natives, Humans and non-humans. Most of the non-humans belonged to the *Desertmoth* tribe. Since Tangai was also called *The Gateway to the North,* one could find members of most tribes, either living in the town or passing through.

Nobody gave us more than a glance when we entered the tavern. All of us were dressed in native garb, the outfits I had picked up from San Deloose in Old Town.

Meadow wore a dark-brown loose robe, which hid her well-formed figure, and she kept her coppery hair tucked under a high, wide-brimmed hat. She hadn't been overly excited about the outfit, since it made her look like a drably old crone, but she didn't have many choices. A married woman without at least a couple of handmaidens traveling in the company of three men was unthinkable, and a lone unattached woman wouldn't travel with three men...unless she was a prostitute, which would make her available to anyone who offered her money.

Therefore, she became a *Windsister*, a holy woman.

The place was quite crowded. In the dim light of the flickering oil lamps, I noticed that a large number of the patrons were non-humans.

"Watch your step," I cautioned my companions, "looks like half the Yellowhorn tribe is assembled in here."

"We've been having some trouble with them lately. They *are* a nasty bunch," Niels DePratt agreed, looking over the short, stocky natives.

My tiny built-in computer registered exactly 27 of them, drinking, eating, gambling, and quarreling. Unlike most other tribes, the males of the Yellowhorns painted their horns with the sap of the *Quar-tree*, which produced a bright, golden color.

The girl who served us was a petite brunette, with a pretty, but sullen face. One of the Yellowhorns laughed as she stopped by his table and put a hand on her breast. When she pushed him away, he slapped her face, grabbed her blouse and ripped it open, exposing her small white breasts.

The girl dropped her tray and crossed her arms over her breasts. Then she ran to the back of the room and disappeared through a door.

Even in the dime light, I had seen her tears.

The Yellowhorn called something after her, while his companions slapped their thighs, hooting and laughing. He stood up, following the girl, grinning hugely.

I didn't like his face and when he walked past, I casually put out a foot, tripping him. He spit like an angry *Marsh-Dragon*, his arms flailing as he tried to regain his balance. Smashing into another table, he managed to stay off the floor.

Too bad, I would have liked to see him roll in the dust.

"My apology, friend," I said, making the sign, but with too much emphasis.

Glaring, he came towards our table, one hand on the hilt of his *kiso*, a long bladed knife with split points.

"I don't accept your apology," he bellowed, drawing his weapon. With a vicious swipe of his right arm, he aimed for my face, but I moved back ever so slightly. The wicked points missed by a fraction...5 mm, to be exact. I felt the rush of cool air on my cheek.

I fell off my chair, but in such a way that I managed to kick the Yellowhorn in the groin. It looked like a clumsy accident.

Screaming hoarsely, he doubled over. Unfortunately, his chin hit the edge of my chair, knocking him out cold.

When his companions picked him off the floor, one of them turned towards me, his *kiso* half drawn, but a couple of burly men, who quietly appeared beside him, cold steel in their hands, stopped him. "It was a fair fight," one of them growled. "Don't dishonor your friend." He looked at me and said softly, "Thanks, I saw what you did."

I shrugged. "It was an accident. I was very lucky."

He grinned. "Come, I'll buy you a drink. That was my daughter. I am Cerbus."

I invited him to our table and introduced my companions. He gave Meadow only a quick glance. Most people were uneasy in the presence of *Windsisters*, and even a little afraid of them, which was the reason I had chosen that particular disguise for her.

Spotting his daughter coming back into the room, he waved her over and ordered drinks. She gave me a shy smile, but said nothing. Cerbus looked after her, when she went to get the drinks and sighed. "I hate to see her work in this place. It's all she can do, she's not too bright, you know. At least here I can keep an eye on her." He stared at the Yellowhorns, and I could see the hatred in his gray eyes. "They're savages, and I'll be glad when they move on."

"Where are they headed?" I asked.

He shrugged his beefy shoulders. "Who knows. I've heard they'll be joining the next caravan up north. They've talked about the *Holy War* that's coming. They want to rid Shantra once and for all of the Demons from the Sky."

"Would their destination be somewhere in the Strathon-mountains?" Niels DePratt asked.

Cerbus looked at him, somewhat surprised. "How do you know?"

"We've heard stories, too," Pratt answered, "and some of them are quite disturbing."

"Like what?"

"They may not only be after the Terrans."

"Pah!" Cerbus waved his big hand and leaned back in his chair. "The Yellowhorns are only a small tribe."

"That maybe so," Darl Mitas said, "but what if they join forces with other tribes?"

We were interrupted by the girl who brought our drinks and platters of grilled *Gandor*. Cerbus drained his glass and got up from his chair. "I'd better get back to work." He looked at me. "I never asked you. Are you planning to join the caravan going north?"

"Yes," I said.

For the first time he looked fully at Meadow, who had said nothing during all this time. The fingers of his left made fluttering motions in the air. "I shall ask a great favor of you, Mother. I have a sister who lives in Neh-mar, the first city north of Dangar. Will you take my daughter with you and deliver her to my sister? I have none I could trust."

I held my breath. Damn it! Meadow had no way out.

She inclined her head, hesitating only for a moment. "I shall be pleased to do this small service for you. The great *Wind-Goddess* will look favorably upon me."

He bowed and smiled. "Her name is Aika."

I cursed silently, watching him walk away. Me and my brilliant ideas! We would have been better off if Meadow had become a prostitute.

She gave me a kick under the table and I grinned without humor. Because we had become so close, her mind was tuned to mine and she knew my thoughts most of the time.

"Don't blame me!" she whispered fiercely. "It's entirely your own fault." Her lips changed into a mocking smile. "You seem to make a career out of collecting young girls."

* * * *

The caravan master was a big brute of a man. Where his left eye had been, he displayed only an empty socket. The left side of his long face was a mass of ugly, horrible scars.

He was a *Gourma*, a half-breed. The horns on his head were short and malformed.

Not many unions between humans and the original natives were fruitful, and when they were, not very desirable.

The *Gourma* were shunned by both sides, not belonging to either, and most children didn't make it past puberty. As soon as they were old enough to be challenged, they usually died in a fight. The ones who survived were feared and respected.

He called himself Falcor. The beast he rode looked as vicious and fearful as its master.

When he checked our riding animals, he nodded with satisfied grunts. "They are in excellent health," he said with a gravelly voice. "You should have no problems."

After much haggling we eventually agreed on a price, still outrages, but we didn't have much of a choice. Dangar was not a safe country, and nobody traveled through it alone.

We left Tangai two days after our arrival there. There was another caravan scheduled to leave in another week, and Cerbus had suggested we join up with them, since he didn't trust Falcor, but we were in a hurry. His daughter, Aika, was only too eager to come with us. She seemed very shy and didn't speak much, but I didn't think she was quite as innocent or simple as he made her out to be.

The caravan master assigned her a space on one of the sleds; covered platforms, carried on the backs of four beasts of burden. There was a group of eight young girls on the same sled, brides on their way to join their eagerly awaiting future husbands. They traveled under the protection of an agent. Somehow I suspected they were slaves on their way to a slave market, and their so-called protector nothing but a slimy slave trader.

Meadow rode beside me when the caravan pulled out. "I guess you've noticed our friends?" she said in a low voice.

I had noticed. The Yellowhorns were part of the caravan. They kept to themselves mostly, but one could not overlook their presence. It was not unusual for even a large group such as theirs to travel with a caravan.

Small groups of Humans and non-humans, most of them merchants accompanying their goods and wares, made up the rest of the travelers. Some of them were mercenaries on their way to a new master.

Then there were Falcor's men; a motley bunch of cutthroats and fortune hunters. I wouldn't trust them if my life depended on it.

A fiery red glow in the east announced the sun, which began creeping slowly into the cloud-covered sky. From past, almost forgotten experience, I knew we'd probably be hit by a sandstorm within the next couple of days. The dry season was almost upon us and sandstorms were quite frequent at this time of year. Not a very good time to travel across the desert.

At first, we followed the river Ran, a tributary of the River Tan. We traveled easily across the flat and fertile land. We entered the province of Dangar about two hours after sunrise, and gradually the countryside became more rugged and hostile. By noon, the mountainous terrain made it impossible to travel along the bank of the river, and the caravan made a sharp turn towards west.

The vegetation became sparse, until it gradually disappeared. Soon we saw nothing but sand around us. We were heading north now towards the Strathon-mountains.

Came nightfall we were all tired and sore. We slept near our riding beasts, covered with blankets against the chill of the night.

The soft sand made traveling much slower the second day.

The storm, which I had expected, hit us shortly before sunset. Falcor's men had already unhitched the large beasts and the seven sleds were resting on the ground. Every rider was responsible for his own animal. We tied our four steeds to the sled in which Aika had been riding. I wanted to stay close to her and suggested that Meadow join her inside the protection of the covered sled. At first, she refused, but when I pointed out that Aika was her charge, she reluctantly climbed into the tent.

The storm blew from the west. A group of sand dunes protected us from the brunt of the storm, and yet, it didn't take long before a layer of sand covered us with a thick blanket. Our animals were scared and snorting furiously, but they kept their heads low, while facing in the direction of the strong wind. The best shelter for us humans was to stay close to the animals. Covered up by our capes, we huddled close to the ground.

The sand hurt as it hit our backs, and nobody was foolish enough to talk. Besides getting a mouthful of sand, it would have been impossible to hear anything above the howling of the wind.

We could do nothing else but wait out the storm.

Once I thought I heard a wailing sound, but when I tried to tune in on it, I heard nothing but the snorting of the animals and the roaring of the storm.

The sandstorm raged on for hours. It finally died down during the night.

A barely audible voice spoke suddenly from the tiny speaker implanted behind my ear.

"Dan. Trouble. Come."

Meadow. She sounded quite urgent.

I told Mitas and DePratt to stay put and slid into the tent. Meadow met me at the entrance. It was pitch-black inside. I waited until my eyes adjusted to night vision. Meadow's hand felt cool inside mine, as she slowly led me to the rear of the sled's interior. I could see the other girls huddled together, except for Aika. She squatted beside a dark shape on the floor.

There wasn't much room for the passengers. Large bundles of all kinds of merchandise took up most of the space.

The shape on the floor turned out to be a man. I recognized him as the man who was supposedly the protector of these girls. His slack face told me that he was dead. Meadow's black conical hat lay beside him. She brushed her red hair out of her face when she looked at me. Her right cheek showed an ugly bruise.

"The bastard tried to rape me," she whispered fiercely.

I had to grin, in spite of the grave situation. "I guess he had no respect for the sacred virgin-hood of this Windsister."

She shot me an angry glance. Her eyes were very large. She had natural night vision, another one of her talents. "I'm in no mood for your jokes," she said, keeping her voice low. She looked at the girls. "What the hell are we going to do with them?"

It was my turn to curse. Now we were stuck with nine girls. We weren't really responsible for any of them, but Meadow knew too well, that I wouldn't abandon them. Their fate would be worse than death.

We may have little choice, with so much at stake.

"Did you have to kill him?" I asked.

"Yes. He knew I wasn't who I appear to be."

"How? He couldn't even see you in here."

Without a word, she handed me something. A pair of goggles. "These were not manufactured on this primitive planet," she said.

I nodded. "Sure wasn't. These are *Nighteyes*."

"The bastard sneaked in here wearing these damn things. By the time I realized it, he was almost upon me. In a way, it is my fault. It was so hot and sticky in here, so I had made myself comfortable."

She didn't have to tell me more. Her robe hung open in the front, revealing her naked creamy body underneath. The brown nipples of her free-swinging breasts peeked at me from their uncovered hiding place.

No Windsister would ever make herself that comfortable.

"He may have been after Aika, but when he saw your delectable exposed body, he apparently changed his mind. Can't say I blame him."

She smiled and touched my cheek. "You're impossible, Dan, but I guess that's why I love you."

Knowing that the other girls couldn't see us, I stepped closer and pulled her to me. Cupping one of her breasts, I squeezed it gently. At first, she tried to push me away, but then she clung to me for a brief moment and melted into my embrace. I kissed her hungrily and released her with a heavy sigh. This was neither the time nor place.

"We have to get rid of him," I said. "Shouldn't be much of a problem."

While Meadow talked to the girls, I hoisted the dead man over my shoulder and carried him outside. Luckily, none of the moons was visible. Heavy clouds still hung low in the sky. Switching off my night vision for a moment, I tested the darkness and found it still complete.

Getting rid of the body proved quite easy. I just dumped him a few feet away from the sled and covered him with sand.

When it came to killing a man without visible telltales, Meadow was very efficient indeed.

Chapter Twelve

A sunny day greeted us next morning. I woke groggy and tired, with hard grains of sand between my teeth. Looking around, I saw animals and humans alike crawling from underneath the thick blanket of almost dust-like sand. The camp came alive with the trumpeting and snorting of the beasts and the curses of the men.

I could see the slave trader's corpse half-buried in the sand, but nobody seemed to take notice. One of Falcor's men finally found him and, after a brief examination, dragged him across the sand to bury him a shallow grave outside the camp. He wouldn't stay buried long anyway, with the forever-moving sand. Besides, there were plenty of carrion eaters around looking for food.

The caravan master rode up shortly after, his scarred face an unreadable mask. "I guess you've noticed the demise of one of your fellow travelers?"

"Yes," I said. "It was a terrible storm."

He gave me a curious look. "No worse than any other," he said.

I shrugged. "He may not have been aware of the danger. Ill fortune for those young brides. They are left without a protector."

The scarred side of his face twitched slightly. "They will be taken care of. It is not your problem."

I let my hands flutter in a sign of great concern. He couldn't ignore it. "Oh yes, it is," I said. "The girls have hired my services, and I have accepted this great responsibility."

"So you have," he said, his good eye glaring. He clicked his left fingers angrily and pulled on the reigns of his beast. "We leave shortly. Make sure you are ready." His beast reared and kicked up a cloud of dust.

I grinned after him. He may be a *Gourma*, but he had honor.

That night the Strathon Mountains were clearly visible, but still far away. This time we made camp without the protection of any sand dunes, but the wind was calm and the sky clear. The stars were

79

visible, and I lay on my back, staring at the familiar constellations. The sign of the *Firehawk* stood high in the zenith, pointing west. I had been there, on Custer, a planet that circled the fiery sun, which was the eye of the hawk.

A hell-world. A place where no human should walk. I lost a good friend there, the only real friend I made while among the stars. He died horribly in the embrace of a poisonous half-sentient plant-thing, something that appeared to him in the shape of a lovely, luscious naked woman. Before any of us could warn him, he ripped off his protective suit in a frenzy of lust and threw himself into the inviting arms and thighs of the pseudo-woman.

I can still hear his screams and see his twisted face when, instead of finding ecstasy and bliss, his sex-organ dipped into a vessel filled with acid poison and his lips dissolved into a bloody mush, as they touched the lovely smiling mouth.

Marco Bandini. We had been a team, two invincible supermen. That's what we thought. Custer taught us different.

We could die, just as easily and fast as any other man, maybe faster.

On Custer, I encountered the Stardogs for the first time. One of our exploration teams accidentally stumbled onto their base and disappeared shortly after. The report of the discovery was their last transmission.

They sent us to Custer to find out what happened to the team. We found the wreckage of their scout ship in the jungle. No survivors. No corpses.

There wasn't much left of the Stardogs' base, but we did find traces of their passing, among them half-eaten carcasses of local animals. It looked as if they had been slaughtered in some kind of ritual, or maybe dissected.

Then we found the human skull.

I fell into an uneasy slumber and awoke groggy. Before I came completely awake, I knew something was wrong.

Opening my eyes, I stared into the familiar grinning visage of a Yellowhorn. Behind him stood a dozen more.

"Justice is always done," he said. His Ginsa-staff pointed at my chest. A cry from the sled told me what happened, and Meadow's warning in my ear came just a bit too late.

The Yellowhorns wouldn't touch a Windsister, but she couldn't stop them from harming Aika and the other girls.

One of the Yellowhorns pushed a girl ahead of him through the entrance of the sled.

Aika.

She gave a small cry, stumbled and fell into the sand. Her captor grabbed her roughly and pulled her to her feet.

Two others appeared, leading Meadow between them.

I groaned when I saw her, stark naked, except for her bracelets and a narrow belt around her waist.

"No Windsister, this one," one of them growled, "unless they've changed their ways."

The one in front of me gave a barking laugh. "The *Great Ones* are good to us. They provide us with not only one, but many maidens today. The *Sky Gods* will be pleased."

I looked for my two companions and found them trussed up beside their riding-beasts.

Great help they were!

Meadow stared at me, waiting for some king of signal, and then her eyes followed my gaze towards Aika, who stood, shoulders drooping in front of her captor. There wasn't much we could do at the moment without endangering the girl.

Looking around, I saw Falcor's men going about their business as usual. No sign of the caravan master anywhere. The bastard probably knew what went on. We couldn't expect any help from that side. The other travelers were either not interested or too scared to interfere.

"There are places where the color of yellow is not a sign of great bravery," I said, crossing two fingers of my left hand.

The one confronting me spat onto the sand, clucking angrily. He pushed his Ginsa-staff deep into the ground and slapped his shoulders. "I am a great warrior and so are my companions. We all carry the sign of the Yac." He bared his chest to show me the scars where the great bird had left its mark.

I made a fist with my left hand, my thumb pointing at the sun. His yellow eyes narrowed and he gave an angry hiss. "You mock me?" he growled. "You don't believe these scars?"

Laughing, I wriggled my fingers, "Perhaps they were made by an unwilling old woman, when you tried to force yourself between her buttocks."

He roared and ripped out his *kiso*. "You hornless smooth-skinned *Eater of boiled Gar-turd*. Any woman in my tribe would willingly and gladly squat down for me. Do you know who I am?"

The others were watching us closely, but none of them made any moves to interfere. From this I knew I faced no common warrior. He wore two clan-rings in his right ear, proclaiming him an honorary member of yet another tribe.

"I am Plactor, Son of Placcar, and nephew to the *Great Wir* Callawhan."

I didn't let my surprise betray me. Callawhan had been an upstart rebel leader, when I lived with the Stag-clan. The *Great Wir* indeed. Seems he moved up in the world while I had been away.

"If you are what you say you are you wouldn't draw your *kiso* on an unarmed man."

He threw the wicked blade to the ground and contemptuously turned his bristled back to me. As I cautiously rose to my feet, he turned and sprang at me with the fluid movements of a *Mountain-Gar.*

On purpose, I didn't move aside, just turned slightly and rammed my left elbow into his chest. I grabbed one of his horns with my right hand, and then we were rolling on the ground.

He was extremely strong, like all of his kind, and an ordinary man would have stood no chance. However, I wasn't an ordinary man. I could have killed him easily in a moment, but I couldn't let them know my strength, so I took his blows. Snarling, he tried to sink his long teeth into my throat, and almost succeeded.

When his sharp nail gauged a deep furrow into my back, I became angry. I don't like pain. I slammed him into the ground. He came up, bellowing with rage and reached for the *kiso* he had so bravely abandoned before.

Swinging the double-pointed weapon in an arc in front of him, he advanced again. He was wary now, but I tired of the game. I let him come closer, and chopping down hard, I grabbed his arm and pulled it behind his back. He roared in pain and kicked backwards. I took him into a full nelson and rammed his head into the sand. Putting my knees into his back, I held him down until he stopped struggling.

I let go and turned him over onto his back. I didn't want to kill him...yet. He lay there, his face slack, but he was breathing.

Chapter Thirteen

We traveled east all day, into the mountains. By nightfall, we left the desert behind and rode among low-growing shrubbery and stunted dried-up trees.

Plactor had been furious when he came to, but he lost a fair fight and had to leave it at that...for the moment, but I knew he'd try to kill me at his first opportunity.

They didn't even tie us up, those arrogant bastards. Then again, where could we go after escaping?

They left the girls under Falcor's protection. The caravan master had politely insisted, with his henchmen standing behind him, their hands casually touching their weapons. Outnumbered, the Yellowhorns rode away, clucking and spitting angrily.

I watched my companions, as they dismounted. DePratt looked haggard and withdrawn. Darl Mitas slumped to the ground and lay there, breathing the cool air in great gulps. The trip had been hardest on him. He displayed an ugly purple bruise on the left side of his head, and he suspected a couple of broken ribs where the blunt end of a Ginsa-staff had left its mark.

Meadow walked over to him, searched in one of her belt pockets and slipped something into his mouth. Moments later Darl relaxed and touched her arm. "You're a terrific woman, you know," he said and grinned, while looking at her exposed breasts.

She chuckled, pulling her robe closer around her naked body. "You men are all alike. There is only one thing on your mind, even if you're on your last breath," she said, but she smiled down at him, her hand holding his.

A little bit too long, for my taste.

She looked at me, scowling.

I grinned foolishly and slid off my mount. The Yellowhorns left us to ourselves. They were settling down for the night, with only one of them on guard.

Poor fools! We could have killed all of them easily in their sleep.

Again, I lay awake, staring into the night sky. Waiting. Contact finally came, almost the instant I expected it.

"Major?" The voice came softly from the implanted speaker behind my ear.

I arose silently and slipped by the guard.

They were waiting for me two hundred meters to the west, in the protection of a small forest.

"How are things coming along, Major?" Kelsey asked. He was a small man, but his size belied his strength. He had undergone the same treatment I had, just like Cherryh, Wu and Killic. The men had been following us since we left Tangai."

"Things are coming along just fine." I smiled at them.

They smiled back, tipping there helmets.

"That bunch giving you any trouble, sir?"

"Nothing I can't handle, so far." I looked at Killic. "Sergeant, I want you to ride back to the ranch and get the skimmer, bring it to this location and wait. I have a feeling we might need you and the skimmer fast and soon." I turned my attention to the others. "The rest of you follow us, but not closely."

Under their capes, I could see the glint of their metallic uniforms and the bulges of weapons. With these four men and their advanced weaponry, I could easily take over this planet. If the local governments knew whom they had invited, they'd probably be scared out of their minds. However, we had no such ambitions. A backwards planet like Redsky had nothing to offer.

Except the Stardogs were here, and we wanted them.

I left them in the forest after I filled them in on all that had happened and walked back to the camp.

The going was rough the next day as we headed deeper into the mountains. It wasn't exactly a road that we followed, but it was obvious that many had passed this way before us.

That night we spent among low, stunted trees. A cool wind blew from the north, and Meadow crawled into the sleeping bag with me. I didn't mind. She kissed me, but gently moved my hand away when I touched her breast. "Not now," she whispered. I sensed her smile. "Save it until we get back safely."

The next morning was crisp and cold, but by late afternoon the wind shifted westerly, and with the shift came the heat.

We crossed a river in the evening. Since the water wasn't very deep and the river narrow, we didn't have to coax our riding animals too much to walk into it. Actually, they were quite eager to take the plunge into the cool, refreshing liquid.

After crossing the river, we rode for another two hours. Gradually the land changed. The ground seemed to be much more fertile and the trees grew straighter and higher. Soon we were traveling amidst a thick forest.

Then we left the trees behind and entered a lush valley.

Another river wound its way through it, and it didn't surprise me when I saw the small town. Actually, town was not the right word. Village would be more descriptive. A dirt-packed road and possibly twenty houses, none of them big.

I noticed small, cultivated fields surrounding the village, a settlement of farmers, hunters, and fishermen.

Everything looked peaceful, if one overlooked the alien structure in the middle of the village. It was cone-shaped, black, and ugly as hell, not something that belonged to this beautiful valley.

It didn't even belong to this planet.

If one still had the impression this was a peaceful place, the hundreds of pyramid shaped tents sitting in the grass-covered area behind the village and the thousands of natives moving between them, shattered that illusion.

Of course, I had detected their presence already some time ago. The clamor of a few thousand warriors can be heard a long time before they are seen.

"It seems we have arrived," Darl Mitas muttered.

Niels DePratt stared silently at the tents and at the alien structure. "That thing scares the hell out of me," he cursed after awhile. "More than those blood-crazed natives."

Plactor grinned at us and wiggled his thumb. "Soon you will find out why you should fear us, Terra-men. This valley will be instrumental in the re-birth of Shantra. We will take back the world that was taken from us a long time ago."

He pulled his mount around and dug his heels into the animal's flanks. The beast screamed and galloped down the trampled road. Waving their Ginsa-staffs, the other Yellowhorns followed. Only one of them stayed back to guard us.

He poked the blunt end of his Ginsa-staff into my ribs. "Go," he said, underlining his words with a rude gesture.

"Let's kill this insolent bastard," Darl Mitas cursed. "We have seen what we came to see."

"No," I said. "Our mission is only just beginning." I ignored the Yellowhorn and spurned my mount to follow Plactor and his companions. After we dismounted, they took our animals away and led us into one of the tents.

They posted a guard to keep us from escaping. Outside, the natives had lit fires and the aroma of roasting meat drifted into the tent.

They were eating and drinking most of the night. A few fights seemed to be breaking out, but otherwise nothing unusual happened.

While the others tried to sleep, I lay awake for some time. In my arms, Meadow fell asleep as if nothing troubled her. I finally drifted off myself.

The sun began to rise already when I opened my eyes again.

* * * *

Meadow, who left the tent for a moment, came back in, spitting like an angry tree-lizard. "That idiot guard out there," she cursed. "After it finally penetrated his thick skull what I needed to do, he insisted I do it right in front of him. When I squatted down he moved behind me and poked something between my buttocks." She spat again. "He almost raped me, the horny bastard, and I nearly killed him. Should have, too."

She gave me a furious look. "Stop grinning! I don't see the humor in this."

"I guess you wouldn't." I chuckled. "But how could he have reacted otherwise, after you invited him to have intercourse with you?"

"I did what?" she gasped. "Now, listen, Griffin…"

When she called me by my last name, she was mad and I refrained from laughing. "Let me explain, Meadow," I said calmly. "Their females squat only when they are in heat and need a male badly."

"So how do they relieve themselves?"

"Just like a male, standing, because they have a penis, like a male, except it is very small and thin." I grinned. "And no balls."

"You're kidding." Meadow stared at me, but then she relaxed and even smiled. "You should have told me, you idiot!" she said accusingly. She smirked. "Do they have breasts?"

I nodded. "They do. Same place you have them. A little different shape, longer, thicker nipples, but otherwise just as soft."

"You ever make love to one of them?"

Oh boy! Question and answer time. When she was in this mood, she wouldn't let me have any peace until she had all the answers.

"I have," I said. "I was very young." No sense hiding it, she'd know.

"Who was she?" Her eyes glowed behind their lenses.

"Threehorn's sister. He was my blood-brother," I tried to explain.

She shrugged, but kept looking at me. "Did you enjoy it? Did she? After all...her species is so different."

"Damn it, Meadow!" I glared at her. "A vagina is a vagina. Yes, I enjoyed it and so did she. And we did it a few times. As long as she was in heat."

"And how long was that?"

I threw up my hands. "Thirty-five days, to be exact."

"Probably not long enough for you. You're always in heat." Her curiosity apparently satisfied, she looked at the half-open entrance. "They seem to be well organized out there and preparing for war. Their weapons aren't as primitive as they should be."

I listened to the crack of exploding shells. Projectile weapons. Primitive, but effective and dangerous.

"You're right," I said "They shouldn't have rifles." Looking through the opening of our tent, I changed the focus of my eyes, zeroing in on one of the warriors in the distance. The image of the rifle he held was sharp and clear...and close. They had done wonderful things to my body. I wasn't even dizzy when I refocused to look at Meadow. "Those rifles are not of Earth-design, nor do they come from any colony of the Terran Empire."

"The Stardogs." She nodded.

"How do you know?" Niels DePratt asked.

I looked at him and then at Darl. Neither one had said anything during Meadow's and my 'discussion', but I had been aware of their uneasiness. I couldn't blame them.

When Meadow became angry, she emanated an emotion of raw fury, which could make strong, fearless men cringe with fear. She had evolved on a fierce planet, and her species had developed many traits to ensure its survival, this ability one of them.

Even I was not immune to her strong emanation. Especially when she wanted to make love, I was putty in her hands, but I could live with that.

"He knows," Meadow answered for me.

"How?"

She smiled. "He's been rebuilt, remember. Your friend is probably less human than those savages out there."

"I wouldn't go as far as making a statement like that," I protested. "They may have changed a few things here and there, but I still feel human, at least inside I do."

She looked at me. "I really don't care, Dan," she said softly and came close. "I'm sorry I blew up like that, but I feel just miserable. I could use a bath and so could you." She wrinkled her nose and put a finger against my lips. "But I still love you. Laughing, she backed out of my reaching arms.

Darl Mitas joined me at the entrance. He watched the natives with great interest. "I can see some kind of structure. It looks like an altar."

"That's probably what it is," I said and glanced at Meadow. "The universal custom before warriors go into battle is to sacrifice a virgin to the war-gods."

"They're out of luck," Meadow said, smiling. "No virgins here."

"Most tribes on Shantra are not too particular about that," I said.

"It seems to me they'll have a virgin after all," Niels commented dryly. He stood beside Darl and pointed at a large group of riders coming down the slope.

More Yellowhorns.

Some of their riding-beasts carried two riders. I looked closer and saw what Niels meant. "The girls!" I swore loudly. "They've attacked the caravan and got the girls. Damn it!"

"What'll they do with them?" Meadow asked.

"Hard to say. The Yellowhorns are unpredictable. First, there is probably going to be a gang rape. One or two of the lucky ones will bleed to death on the altar. All will be roasted and eaten."

"That's barbaric."

I shrugged. "They are savages and they love human meat, especially human female meat. Smoked breast is their favorite."

Meadow glared at me. "Stop it, Griffin! You make me sick."

"I'm only giving you the brutal facts, Meadow. Don't act so shocked. You've seen worse."

She sighed. "Yes, I have. But it still makes me ill."

"We might all be on the menu," Darl said. "Didn't you tell me those aliens, the Stardogs, eat humans?"

"From the evidence we've seen it seems that way," I said. I was watching a group of newcomers. One rider, taller and bigger than the others, drew my attention. He looked familiar, and then I recognized him. Callawhan. The *Great Wir,* as Plactor had called him. Older and bigger, but I would have known his ugly visage anywhere.

The rebel-leader had arrived.

I became conscious of Meadow looking at me. "The presence of those girls changes the situation somewhat, doesn't it, Dan?" she said softly.

I nodded. "You're right, it does complicate matters. So does the arrival of Callawhan." I pointed him out. "He knows me from way back. We were never great friends. Fact is he hates my guts."

"Beautiful," I heard Darl mutter. He gave a deep sigh. "I should have known this would be no easy mission, not with a guy like you, Griffin."

"Thank you, old friend." I chuckled and walked out of the tent.

Time to get some answers.

Chapter Fourteen

Callawhan watched me as I walked towards him. He barely glanced at the guard, who had tried to step in my way, now lying unconscious.

"Dan Griffin," he said, his left hand moving across his face. "I prayed to the mountain-gods some day we'd meet again."

I grinned, repeating the gesture. At least he gave me a warrior's greeting. "The mountain-gods and the *Movers of Fate* seem to have answered your prayers, *Great Wir*."

His leathery face showed no expression, but I could see the surprise in his yellow eyes. "You know?" he asked.

"I have met your nephew." I smiled, weaving a pattern with my fingers.

"Plactor!" he grunted, stabbing angrily at the air. "Think twice!" His hand slashed down hard.

I had to suppress a loud laugh. Think twice indeed. Apparently, the Great Wir Callawhan didn't think much of his loudmouthed nephew.

The rebel leader leveled his Ginsa-staff at me. A smile flickered over his wide, thin-lipped mouth. "You are a prisoner, Dan Griffin," he stated. "When we met last it was I who was in that position."

I shrugged. "As I said, the Movers of Fate seem to favor you. For now. Who knows what happens next? Who controls the future?"

"I control what happens next," he said. His hand made a sweeping gesture. "More than five thousand warriors who will follow me into the Holy War. I am Callawhan, the Great Wir. Future generations will hail me as the *Liberator of Shantra*."

"Five thousand warriors is not really a large force, Great Wir." I smiled. "Unless you have more stowed away in a secret hiding place?"

Callawhan stared at me, his leathery face a mask, and then suddenly he gave a barking laugh. "A secret hiding place? Very good, Dan Griffin. Yes, we may have exactly that." The gaze of his yellow eyes locked on the alien structure. "You have seen and you know. You are no fool. We have mighty allies. Their weapons are superior to yours. They promised us help."

"What do they want in return?" I asked.

"In return?"

It was my turn to laugh. I made a waving motion in the air. "You can't be that ignorant, Callawhan. The Stardogs, as we call your new friends, are no charitable benefactors. They will demand payment, and you may not be able to pay the price."

Callawhan's hand chopped down three times. "That is the problem with you Terra-men. You always talk about payment, trade. You take our land, our rivers, our forest, and still you want more." Clucking angrily, he pointed at the black cone. "They took nothing, asked for nothing."

"So what do they want, Great Wir?" I asked mildly.

"To help. To rid Shantra of the presence of the Terra-men," he hissed, his yellow eyes afire. "They will give us weapons, train our warriors, and stay until the Holy War is over. Then they will leave." His hand chopped down again. "But I tire of this conversation, Terra-man. Go back into your prison until I call for you. You've talked about payment? There is still a debt we will have to settle."

Pulling hard on the rein of his beast, he forced it to claw the air. It screamed in defiance, digging up dirt with its huge clawed feet. After giving it free rein, he galloped down the slope, followed by his warriors.

I hadn't looked at the captive girls. There wasn't anything I could do now anyway. The girl Aika looked at me with pleading eyes and as she passed me she called out, "Help us, please!" She was frightened to death and I couldn't blame her.

Damn it! She should have stayed with her father in Tangai, where she was pawed only occasionally by drunken patrons.

Two of the Yellowhorns stayed behind and prodded me with their Ginsa-staffs. I had in mind to pull them off their beasts, but then I let them herd me back to the tent.

"Great conversation you had," Meadow commented. "What did you actually accomplish?"

"More than you think," I said. "By making him aware of my

presence I have bought us some time. Years ago, I did something that he will never forget. He is out for revenge, and he is going to challenge me. His honor demands it."

"He is a very dangerous foe, Major Griffin," Niels DePratt said. "Vicious, cunning, and exceptionally strong. He may be one of the greatest warriors that ever lived on Shantra. He will surely kill you."

I saw Meadow smiling. "You still don't understand, DePratt," she said. "Dan Griffin is no ordinary man, not anymore. He could probably wipe out half of that army out there and walk away without a scratch."

DePratt shook his head, giving her a crooked smile. "Surely you overestimate your friend's abilities. Even if his body has been altered, he is still flesh and blood. He can still die."

"I can die," I broke in, "but I am not easy to kill." I gave Meadow a warning look. She understood and nodded slightly.

The lieutenant had been briefed about me, of course, but much he didn't know and would never know.

In many ways, I was one of the Empire's secret weapons in the fight against the Stardogs, and it made no sense to reveal more than necessary. Besides, I didn't trust Lt. Niels DePratt.

"What did you do to that Callawhan that makes him hate you so much?" Meadow asked.

"It's a long story," I answered, "and it goes way back. I was maybe sixteen or seventeen years old and living with the Stag-clan, as I used to occasionally. One day a young warrior, a Yellowhorn, came looking for a female. You see, among the tribes females are traded frequently to bring in fresh blood. He was quite a loudmouth, claimed to have killed who knows how many enemies, most of them Terra-men, of course. He bragged that some day he would be a great leader and would unite all of the tribes to fight a Holy war."

"Callawhan?" Meadow said.

"Right." I nodded. "He desired Threehorn's sister."

Meadow smiled. "I understand. The same one you…?" She left the sentence unfinished, but smirked as I continued.

"I challenged him, but since I did not carry the sign of the Yac-bird, I was not classified as a warrior. So Threehorn, who was older than me, and my blood-brother, took over the challenge." I looked at Niels DePratt. "You called Callawhan a great warrior. He was nothing compared to Threehorn."

"I knew him," Niels DePratt muttered, a shadow darkening his eyes.

"You did?" I asked, surprised.

"He was a troublemaker, that's all I know of him."

"Then you didn't know him very well, Lieutenant. Threehorn had the making of greatness inside him. Whatever Callawhan claimed he would do, Threehorn would have done. He had a dream, and his greatest dream was to have peace among the tribes and peace with the settlers. New-wave and Old-wave." I swallowed hard, as memories flooded up inside me. "Then some bastard murdered him, and some day I'll find out who!"

DePratt avoided my eyes and Darl put his hand on my arm. "Easy, Dan."

Only now I realized I had been shouting.

"Sorry," I murmured, "but he was more than just a friend, I loved him like he was my flesh and blood brother."

"What about Callawhan?" Meadow asked.

"Callawhan?" I said. "Well, he turned out to be a real great hero. He backed out of the challenge and left with his tail tucked between his legs."

"And that's why he hates you?"

"That was the first time we met. The last time I saw him we caught him trying to steal a herd of riding animals from the Stag-clan. It was I who spotted him and a couple of his followers as they sneaked into the tribe's grazing grounds. Instead of killing him, they tied him naked and weaponless into a Yac-bird's nest. Ironically, Threehorn's sister took pity on him and sneaked out at night to free him. She squatted down for him, but after they had coupled, he beat her and sent her back to her tribe."

"Not a very nice fellow, that one," Meadow commented dryly.

"Threehorn was very angry and swore to kill Callawhan, but he never got the chance anymore."

"Sad story, Griffin," Niels DePratt said. "It all adds up to one thing. Because of your past we are all in big trouble now."

"My past, Lieutenant DePratt, has really no bearing on our present situation," I said icily. "It is that thing," I stabbed at the black, ugly cone-shaped structure, "that thing out there, which causes all these problems, and we better find out what it is and who owns it."

* * * *

I was listening to the guard I had knocked out. He bragged to his friends that he could easily take me in a fight. I had surprised him, that's all. He kept glancing in my direction, certain I couldn't hear him, because he thought I was out of earshot. Had I been a normal Earthman, he would have been correct, but I wasn't. He didn't know about my enhanced hearing.

"I haven't seen anyone from the village," I said to Meadow, who sat beside me on a fallen tree-trunk. "Wonder what happened to the inhabitants."

"Probably dead," Meadow commented.

I shook my head. "As ruthless as they are, I can't imagine they'd murder a whole village."

"I wouldn't mind having a closer look at that thing." Meadow lifted her chin, pointed it at the alien artifact.

"Neither would I. We'll do it tonight."

"What are you two discussing?" someone said behind us.

I turned around to look at Darl. He grinned lopsidedly, holding his chest. "I could use one of those miracle painkillers you gave me a couple of days ago," he said, looking at Meadow.

"Still hurts?" she asked.

"Every time I breathe."

"Take off your shirt," Meadow said. "I'll have a look at it."

He took off his shirt, winced when Meadow probed his chest with gentle fingers. "How's your head?" she asked.

"Better. Still hurts, though."

"Not much I can do about your ribs. I don't think they're broken, just cracked. They'll heal. Here, take one of these."

He swallowed the pill, and then joined me on the fallen tree. "If it weren't for those crazy devils, I'd say it is a beautiful day," he said.

It *was* a beautiful day. Or it had been. The sun began disappearing behind the mountaintops. The day came to an end. More riders had come in during the day, not all of them Yellowhorns. I was itching for action. Meadow and I would go exploring after dark. We had to find out what was inside that black cone...and the fate of the people of this settlement.

As the evening darkened, fires started burning between the tents. The aroma of roasting meat drifted into our noses.

"I hope those are *Gandors* they are roasting," Darl said dryly.

A couple of warriors came to our tent, threw something into the grass in front of me. "The Great Wir sends this," one said, making circles with one finger.

I repeated the gesture. "We are grateful."

I picked the charred chunk of meat from the ground, wiped off the blades of grass sticking to it. It was still hot.

"How are we going to eat that?" DePratt asked.

I ripped off a piece, offered it to him. "With your teeth." I grinned. "Like Darl said, let's hope it is Gandor."

He shook his head. "I'd rather go hungry."

Meadow took the piece of meat from my fingers and bit into it.

I knew it was Gandor-meat. I'd eaten it many times before. Exactly like this.

"Not bad," Meadow said. "A little too raw for my taste."

They had left us our canteens and we washed the meat down with stale water.

"Maybe you're not human anymore, after all," DePratt commented, watching us with disgust.

Darl chuckled. "Griffin never was really human. He spent half of his life with the Stag-clan. If Lane hadn't come along he probably would have married Threehorn's sister."

The mention of Lane didn't exactly lift my mood. About Threehorn's sister? It was true, I had liked her, maybe even loved a little. We coupled, and the thought that I might have chosen her as my mate, was not farfetched.

Meadow gave me an anxious look. Damn her and her empathic ability.

"You never told me her name," she said softly.

"Blue Petal. She loved the blue flowers of the *Mountain-creeper*."

"How romantic. Did you love her?"

"Damn it, Meadow!" I glared at her. "How would I know? I was fifteen years old. Can we drop this? We've been through this before."

She laughed. "You loved her. I'm glad to hear that you had a heart at one time."

"What does that mean?"

"Forget it, Griffin!" Her eyes glowed behind their lenses.

"What is your problem, Meadow?"

She shrugged. "Nothing. Like I said before, just feeling miserable. The noise those savages are making, the reek of smoke and burning meat, the inactivity, it is getting to me. I'm itching for action."

"You'll get it tonight. Be patient."

"I'm talking about other action," she said with a low voice, lowering her lashes. But then she laughed and took another bite from her piece of meat.

I chuckled. "You *are* a teasing bitch."

The way her moods changed always amazed me, but then again, she wasn't really human.

Darl cleared his throat beside us. "If you two are done with your lover's quarrel, maybe you'd like to look at this?"

"We're not really quarrelling," Meadow said. "Just having a discussion. What is it you want us to see?"

"I think we're about to have a visitor." He pointed at the darkening sky.

An oval-shaped object was descending swiftly. The light from the setting sun reflected off the glinting hull. The object circled the camp once, and then it landed inside the village.

* * * *

We didn't see where exactly the alien space shuttle had landed, but it wasn't hard to figure out.

I looked at Meadow. She nodded. "You stay here," I told Darl and DePratt.

"What are you planning?" DePratt asked.

"Trying to find out whom we're dealing with."

Our guard was still busy talking with his friends, and it was dark enough to slip away from the camp without being seen by anyone. It took us about five minutes to reach the protection of the first house. We didn't find any signs of the former occupants. This house and all the others were dark.

One of the moons rose in the north, bathing the street with its pale light. We could see the shuttle beside the black structure. A few man-like shapes moved around the shuttle. I adjusted my vision to bring the images closer.

Meadow exhaled sharply beside me, while looking through a small vision-enhancer. "This doesn't make much sense," she whispered. "I didn't know the natives of Redsky were capable of space-travel."

"They're not." I focused on one of the figures. He looked like a Shantra-born, except he didn't dress like one. He wore shiny space garb. "No native to this planet, I'm sure of that," I murmured.

"Somehow I can't image that the Stardogs look like this," Meadow mused. "Then again, I could be wrong. We've never seen one."

"The weapon Commander Ryker showed me was made by a species with three-fingered hands. The guy I'm looking at has four fingers and a thumb."

We stayed in the shadow of the houses as we made our way closer to the shuttle. I counted five males. There could haven been more, either inside the alien structure or in one of the houses. Subdued light streamed through the windows of the house closest to the shuttle. Two of the males went into the house. They came back a short time later.

A woman struggled between them...a human woman. Naked and highly pregnant. Her belly looked huge. She screamed something. Over and over. At first, I couldn't make out the words, because of her uncontrollable sobbing, but then they became clear.

"Take this bastard-thing out of me!"

They dragged her across the dark street and into the black structure. A bright light spilled momentarily out of an oval opening. When it closed it also shut off the woman's screams.

"Now we know that they didn't kill the people of this village," Meadow whispered.

"At least not all of them," I replied.

"That woman was hysterical," Meadow said, her voice tight. "And scared out of her mind."

I nodded. You didn't need to be a mind reader to have deduced that, but Meadow was an empath. She detected emotions with more clarity and certainty than a normal person did, and sometimes it affected her.

"You're alright?" I asked.

"I'm fine." She looked at the house. "There are more inside."

"I wouldn't mind having a look," I said.

All the aliens disappeared into the black building. We hugged the walls of the houses, stayed in the shadow of the trees that grew in the yards, and slowly made our way towards the target-house. When we reached it, we found the door unlocked and we slipped inside.

We were in a small vestibule, the door to the rest of the house stood slightly ajar. Light fell through the narrow crack. Meadow, who was ahead of me, carefully pushed open the door with her foot. I noticed she had drawn her small *Disrupter*, which she had concealed under her robe.

I was weaponless. Or so it seemed.

Meadow stepped through the door, into another room. I followed her slowly, my ears tuned in to the sounds surrounding us. I heard the subdued whisperings of female voices.

The room we entered held fourteen beds, eleven of the occupied by women, all of them naked and highly pregnant.

One of them saw us. She put her hand to her mouth when she looked at me. "Who are you?" she asked with a tremor in her voice.

"There is no-one else here," Meadow said to me, but I had discovered that already.

All the other women had seen us now. Some cried out in surprise.

"Be silent!" Meadow warned them and stepped up to one of the beds. "We are not here to harm you," she said with a low voice.

"Did you come to rescue us?" one asked hopefully.

I joined Meadow. The woman on the bed looked quite young. Her belly was stretched beyond a normal pregnancy, and her once pretty face mottled and puffed up, her hair unkempt.

"What's your name?" I asked her.

"Thami."

"Where are all the men, Thami?"

She shrugged. "Probably dead. We haven't seen them since the natives invaded our town."

"How long ago was that?" Meadow asked.

"Months. I don't know. They keep us in here all the time."

"What is going on?" I hesitated. "I notice you're all pregnant."

She laughed shrilly. "We sure are. But what we carry inside us is not human."

"Explain."

One of the other women slipped from her bed. She came over and sat at the edge of Thami's bed. "They put their young inside our bellies, where they grow. We are in pain all the time."

I swung around when I heard the opening of the outer door. There would not have been enough time to hide, so we just stood there.

Two of the aliens walked in. They stopped when they spotted us. I saw the small weapon in the hand of one of them. "How did you get in here?" He spoke the dialect of the Yellowhorns.

I grinned at him. "Through the door."

"You're a human male," the other one said.

"Very observant."

"What are you doing here?"

"I could ask you the same question."

"You don't ask any questions!" He spoke harshly.

"No action," I whispered to Meadow, but she already knew I was going to say that.

"You!" The one with the weapon pointed it at me. "Come with us!"

He stepped aside to let me pass. "Where are you taking me?" I asked.

"No questions!" he barked.

"I'm a friend of Callawhan. He will be angry."

"Callawhan has no human friends. Go!" He shoved his weapon between my ribs. He didn't know how close he came to dying, but there was still time for that.

We walked across the street, headed for the black structure. The door hissed open and I stepped into a brightly lit corridor. It spiraled upwards. We walked through another door, and then we entered a small room. It held four bunks, three of them occupied. They pushed me into the room. The door closed behind me.

I looked around my prison cell. It was bare, except for a small cube in one corner. A hole in the top of the cube revealed its nature.

Only one of the figures sat up, two bleary eyes stared at me out of an unshaven face. "What happened to Torris?" he asked in a weak voice.

I shrugged. "I don't know. Just got here."

"Who are you?"

"My name is Griffin. Yours?"

"I am Kruller. That there is Martan, and he is Perto."

Perto lifted his head. His eyes were sunken and his face haggard. "I'd like to say I'm happy to see you, Griffin, but I have a feeling you didn't come to rescue us."

"Maybe I did."

The third one, Martan, began laughing, but stopped abruptly, as his body was racked by a fit of coughing. Catching his breath, he croaked, "Pardon me, if I don't get up. My legs are a little wobbly these days."

"What the hell happened here?" I sad down on the empty cot.

All three men looked emancipated, their clothes hung in tatters on their skinny frames.

"You'll find out," Kruller said sullenly. "You poor bastard."

Chapter Fifteen

It didn't take long before they came for me. The two who entered our small prison looked like Shantra-born. I knew they weren't. They spoke the dialect of the Yellowhorns without an accent, but they used only words to communicate.

All Shantra-born spoke in two languages: words and gestures.

These two didn't.

Shoving a small gun into my face, one of them said, "You! Come with us!"

I shrugged and followed the other one through the door. Without looking back, I knew the first one was right behind me. Before the door closed, I heard the weak voice of Kruller, "Good luck, Griffin."

We walked down a narrow corridor, through a door, then up a set of stairs. At the top, I found myself in a large room. A wall made out of a transparent substance gave me a glance into another room.

It looked like a hospital room. There were low tables. On the tables lay naked women, pregnant naked women. Wires and tubes connected them to instruments and long tubes filled with a murky liquid. Shapes in hooded lab-coats moved between the tables.

The shapes were not human, but neither were they Shantra-born. Their faces were hidden inside the hoods, but their legs bent the wrong way.

Even with my enhanced hearing, I could not make out what they were saying. Only muffled voices reached my ears. Then one of the women began screaming. I had no trouble hearing that. I stopped walking. My guards tried to push me along, but I stood, determined to see what was going on in the next room.

The screaming woman thrashed around on the table. I noticed that her arms and legs had been restrained to the table with wide leather straps.

While I watched, I saw the huge belly of the woman ripple with movement from the inside, and then suddenly it burst open, like a ripe melon. Red blood sprayed the two robed figures standing beside her.

Something began to emerge out of the burst belly. All I could see were huge red eyes above a snout full of teeth.

One of my companions chuckled beside me. "Witness the holy moment of another birth."

The woman stopped screaming, her body lay lax on the table.

"I also witnessed the moment of death," I said grimly.

"Not dead, not yet. We're keeping her alive until the hatchling is strong enough to leave the womb. Her body will provide it with nourishment."

"Is this how your species propagates?" I asked.

"That is the way," the other guard said.

I looked one more time at the slime-covered toothy creature inside the woman's ripped belly, and then I turned away and faced him. "Am I correct to assume this is not your true shape?" I asked him.

He laughed and gave me a shove. "You ask too many questions. Now, move!"

They pushed me through another door, into another room. It was furnished with a couple of low, padded benches, a bed, and a few high stools. A counter ran the length of one wall.

"Wait here!"

They left. I made myself comfortable on one of the benches. I noticed another door in the opposite wall. It opened while I looked at it.

I had expected anything, but not this. The person who walked into my room was a tall, slim human woman.

Human and beautiful.

"I am Pihra," she said and handed me a tall transparent tube. "Have they treated you well?"

I grinned at her. "If I overlook the gun that was shoved between my ribs, I'd say, I was treated all right."

She smiled. I could see two long, thin incisors behind her full lips. "You have to admit, you've been snooping where you should not have."

"I am a curious fellow," I said, smiling back at her.

She took a sip from her own tube, looked at me over the rim. I noticed her deep black eyes and the long lashes. "I brought you a peace-offering," she said from behind the tube. The green liquid inside amplified the size of her incisors.

I smelled the liquid, inhaled the sweet fragrance. It reminded me of the cheap liqueur old Miguel had been selling in his tavern.

"It won't harm you," she said, watching me.

Shrugging, I drank from the tall vessel. It actually tasted better than it smelled.

"Empty it," she said, draining hers.

It went down smoothly, but left a tardy aftertaste on my palate. I felt suddenly sexually aroused. When Pihra began to undress, it confirmed my suspicion that the drink had been spiked with something other than just alcohol. She had a lovely body, a narrow waist with flaring hips. Her breasts were high and full, her pubic area free of any hair.

"Take off your clothes," she commanded me.

Dumbfounded, I complied. When I was naked, she pushed me backwards and straddled me. My mind seemed numb. Whatever had been in that drink, it overrode the conditioning I received when they altered my body.

My subconscious screamed *Danger*! but I ignored it.

Cradled by her hot, fleshy thighs my pole slid easily into her warm love channel. She was wet and slippery and the walls of her sex-canal greedily sucked on my pulsing member. Moaning deeply, she lifted up to meet my first thrust. We hammered against each other for a long time. I was furious because I knew what she had done when she gave me that drink and I drove into her with great force.

I exploded inside her, and my own groan of pleasure mixed with her loud cry. Her mouth closed over mine and she kissed me deeply, her tongue snaking into my mouth. Her saliva mixed with mine. It had a strange, but pleasant taste.

She released my mouth, sat up, but kept moving slowly above me. My pole felt still rigid inside her tight, but incredibly soft sheath.

"Don't come yet." She smiled. "We want to enjoy this for a long time."

"Yes," I moaned, my fingers sinking into her large breasts. I squeezed hard, knowing somehow that she liked it.

She began moving with slow, measured strokes. I felt myself swelling inside her as her strong inner muscles squeezed my organ. I grabbed her wide hips and heaved up against her, pushing as deep as I could. Her black eyes locked with mine and, increasing her tempo, she soon gyrated with a blurry motion.

"Yes," I screamed as the pressure built up inside me. My loins were on fire and nothing in the world could have made me pull out of this hot oven of pure pleasure. There seemed to be no end. The pleasure went on and on, and when I finally exploded, I found myself hammering between her widespread thighs.

How and when I came to be on top of her I didn't remember.

She laughed and kissed me again, her saliva flowing into my mouth. I swallowed it down eagerly. Again, my pole, still buried inside her, became rigid.

"Well, well," she chuckled. "You are certainly blessed with endurance and great powers of recuperation." With that, she began to move under me and I felt tears of pleasure running down my face, as she cradled me between her hot thighs.

Somehow, she ended up on top of me again. When I climaxed, she bent forward, opened her mouth, but all I saw were her white perfect breasts swinging in front of my eyes.

With detached interest, I registered the sharp momentary pain, when she sank her fangs into my jugular, automatically measuring the flow of blood.

She could have drained me and I would have done nothing.

* * * *

When I became aware again, I found myself back in the small prison-cell. A pair of bleary eyes peered into mine.

"Kruller?" I said, at least I thought I did, but the voice I heard sounded weak and could have belonged to a *Snow-frog*.

Kruller grinned without humor. "Welcome to Hell, Griffin."

I tried to sit up, fell back onto my bunk when a wave of nausea washed through my body.

"Take it easy," Kruller said. "You need rest."

I shivered, realized I was still naked. "Where are my clothes?"

"Under your bunk." He grinned again. "Don't bother getting dressed. They favor the newcomers."

Managing to sit up, I said, "I saw a woman giving birth to something."

Perto laughed hollowly from his bunk. "I don't believe you were supposed to see that."

"Why not?"

"Because they're very secretive about the way the propagate."

"So what did I see?"

Kruller went back to his bench and sat down. "As much as we can figure out, their females don't carry their own young. They need a surrogate host. Human women are obviously the perfect host."

"Who was that woman I had sex with?" I asked.

All three men laughed, but it didn't sound cheerful. "Woman?" Martan choked out. "Wait until she doesn't bother to take on human form. Wait until she goes for your jugular before she takes you into her belly."

"I know she drank my blood," I said, "but why the sexual intercourse?"

"Because they enjoy it and because they use our semen for their unholy experiments. We know they are Shape Shifters, but they cannot stay very long in the shapes they assume. We believe they are trying to create a sub-species, one that can shift into a certain shape and keep it as long as they wish."

"And the blood?"

"Vampires. They're vampires, bloodsuckers."

I lay back on my bunk, trying to digest what I had heard. Until now our knowledge about the species we called the Stardogs had been limited. It seems I learned more these last twenty-four hours than what we knew about them until now.

Shape Shifters. Vampires. Cannibals.

Possibly also a symbiotic life form, perhaps parasitic.

Apparently, they knew more about us than we did about them.

I needed to talk to Meadow, but when I tried to contact her, I received only static. Somehow it didn't surprise me. Before we entered this building, I attempted to analyze the material of the walls. They consisted of a fusion of metal and some synthetic material, something akin to plastic. Foreign to this planet. It probably blocked any electrical and magnetic impulses trying to penetrate the walls and ceiling.

Though hoping that Meadow was okay and that she had escaped capture, I fell into an uneasy slumber.

Chapter Sixteen

I woke up when rough hands shook my aching body. Groggy and unhappy, I opened my eyes to find a Yellowhorn staring at me. Instantly awake, I reached for this throat, but he was fast, faster than any Yellowhorn should be, and evaded me easily.

Then I remembered where I was.

"What do you want?" I asked, my voice stronger than I had expected it to be.

He grinned at me. With a glance at my three roommates, he said, "Since you're the newest and strongest of our guests, we decided it was your turn, again."

When I reached for my bundle of clothing, which I had used as a pillow, he waived me off. "You won't need that. Come as you are."

Naked, I stumbled ahead of him. My feet seemed like lead and my head felt as if I had been drunk for a week. We walked past the room with the transparent wall, but everything was quiet. When he shoved me into the room with the benches, I found it already occupied.

Pihra and another woman sat on high stools, looking expectantly at the opening door. Pihra dismissed my guard and told me to sit down on one of the benches. "Did you rest well?" she asked.

I shook my head. It seemed about to jump off my shoulders. "I've slept better," I said. "My feet are a couple of anchors and I have a tremendous headache. I hope you don't want to have sex again."

Pihra smiled. "Didn't you enjoy it?"

"If I did I don't remember." Actually, I lied. I had a small, but powerful memory chip inside my skull. It recorded everything I said, saw, heard, and did. I could access it any time I wanted to, but so could others, if they had the right equipment.

"Here, drink this." Pihra held out a tube filled with liquid. I eyed the green substance suspiciously. "Is that the same stuff you gave me yesterday?"

She nodded. "It's a stimulant. Once your body adjusts to it, you will feel better."

Shrugging, and against my better judgment, I emptied the tube. The liquid ran down my parched throat and seemed to have an immediate effect. In a short time, the lethargy left my body and my head felt clear.

However, my penis seemed to be on fire.

The other woman, who had been silent until now, laughed softly when she saw my reaction. "I see you are ready to play."

I looked at her and grinned. "Are you?"

Her long incisors gleamed between purple lips. Without a word, she reached down, grabbed the hem of her thin robe and pulled it over her head, exposing her naked body.

I watched Pihra do the same. Looking at the two nude Valkyries, I heard warning bells going off inside my head, but my urge proved stronger.

"I am Sehla," the second woman said, pushing me onto my back. She bent down and, with a sigh, she put her mouth on the head of my member, her tongue tickling the shiny head. Then very slowly, she swallowed my shaft, until it was buried up to the root in her mouth, sucking on it with gentle force.

She had a way of moving her tongue around my swollen organ. Sometimes her teeth bit down just hard enough to be on the verge of hurting.

Without lifting her head from my lap, she moved on top of me, spreading her thighs over my face. The pink cleft of her hairless pussy hovered close to my mouth. Without thinking, I grabbed her buttocks and pulled her down. When my tongue found her clitoris, she moaned deeply and clamped her thighs around my head. She tasted clean, and the taste of her pussy-juice made me even hornier.

Moaning loudly, her pelvis writhed above my face. She seemed to have several orgasms until I finally reached my own. When I came, she swallowed every drop of my sperm. Even after I was finished, she kept sucking on my shaft. Licking it clean, she lifted her head. "You are still hard," she said. "That is good. Now I want to feel you inside me."

She lay back and spread her legs wide. "Come," she cooed and pulled me on top of her. I was still so hard, and when her soft pussy-walls molded themselves around my pole, I became almost delirious with pleasure. I moved between her widespread thighs like a man who had been without a woman forever. The longer we were locked together, the harder I seemed to become.

Sehla was not only an expert with her mouth, but also a master with her pussy. She knew exactly when to apply pressure and when to release her muscles to keep me from coming too soon.

Even though quite muscular, her body felt soft, her skin like satin. She kissed me deeply, her tongue snaking into my mouth, teasing and tantalizing. I tried to keep my weight off her, but she crushed my body to hers, her soft, full breasts flattening against my chest.

"Don't worry," she moaned. "I like to feel your full weight on me. I can take it." We hammered against each other for a long time. When I climaxed, it came again with tremendous force and I barely felt her fangs piercing my jugular.

I remember vaguely her leaving me and another shadow hovering above me, felt my engorged organ entering another hot vessel. I experienced exquisite pleasure, and then I fell into darkness.

* * * *

Awareness came slowly. Even opening my eyes seemed an effort. Feeling sluggish and drained, I sat up to look around and found myself still in the same room.

I saw someone busy at the counter, someone dressed in a short, hooded robe, with the hood thrown back. I could see the top and back of a skull, no hair, but a mass of long, thin tendrils, like a nest of slowly moving snakes. The legs that were visible beneath the robe were smooth and muscular, ending in split hoofs.

The angle was wrong. These legs didn't have any kneecaps in front.

The creature turned to look at me out of red eyes. It didn't have a nose, just two slits above a slightly protruding jaw. Tiny tendrils covered a pair of thick lips.

The lips opened to reveal white teeth and a pair of long incisors.

"You're awake," the creature said with Pihra's voice.

"Who are you?" I demanded to know, but my voice didn't come out with the commanding edge I had put into it. Rather, it sounded like the squeak of a fledgling Yac-bird.

A very cheery human laugh escaped the creature's mouth. "I am Pihra. Does this form offend you?"

I swallowed a couple of times, cleared my throat and was surprised how almost normal my voice sounded when I spoke. "No more than mine does you."

She laughed again and walked towards me. Standing in front of me, she opened her robe to let me look at the rest of her.

I didn't see any breasts on her slim, but muscular body, only a couple of long nipples. I remembered the toothy creature I had seen crawling out of the woman's ripped belly. No mother would want to put parts of her body between those snapping jaws.

However, I studied with interest Pihra's genital region. It looked remarkably like that of a human woman.

She saw my look and chuckled softly. "We create offspring the same way humans do," she said. "And we enjoy it as much."

"Is that your real voice?" I asked.

"One of many," she said. "Mimicking sounds is part of our survival."

"So is shape changing, I suppose?"

She nodded and let her robe fall close again. The hand that held the hem of the robe had three fingers and an opposing thumb.

"What are you doing on Shantra?" I asked, using the native word for Redsky.

"Breeding," she said. "We find humans to be the perfect host-bodies for our offspring."

"But when your offspring are born, they kill the women who give them life."

She smiled at me and shrugged. "They also nourish our young as they struggle through their first stage of their development." She went back to the counter. Taking a couple of vials from a shelf, she studied them intently. "This is very interesting," she said after awhile and turned to look at me. The tiny tendrils around her mouth moved gently and her red eyes were wide open. I noticed that instead of eyebrows she had a prominent bony ridge running from one side of her face to the other.

I looked back at her, but didn't say anything.

"Are you a different species of human?" she asked.

"What do you mean?"

"Your blood, it is human, but there are some additional elements we've never seen. Also, your bones...they are much denser than is normal for a human."

Shrugging, I stared at her. "I was born here on Shantra. Maybe

I'm a mutation."

She shook her head. "No mutation." She came closer. Holding a tiny oval object in her hand, she pressed it against my forehead and ran it down my body. "You have implants in your body," she commented. "Artificial implants." Her red eyes bored into mine. "What are you?"

Before I could answer, she stepped back and reached for something on the counter. Turning to face me again, she pointed it at me. "Don't move!" she said sharply.

I smiled and stood up. "Are you going to kill me?" I asked, taking another step. My head was clear now. The lethargy had disappeared out of my limbs. I knew I would pay for it later, but now was not the time to think about that. I trusted the tiny computer in my chest-cavity to regulate the amount of adrenalin the artificial glands were shooting into my system.

The opening door distracted Pihra momentarily.

I didn't need more than that.

Moving faster than any normal Human could have, I stepped around Pihra, twisted her gun-hand onto her back and took it from her powerless fingers. Not wanting to be hampered by her body, I gave her a push. She fell forward, landed halfway on the bunk I had been lying on.

She screamed to alert the one coming into the room. I turned to confront the intruder. Expecting Sehla, I was surprised to find myself looking at a creature not unfamiliar to me.

A Mountain-skat.

I had hunted the fierce predator often enough in my youth.

Even knowing this animal could not be real, not here, I knew the danger was not imaginary. Jumping back, I turned to face another one of them. Snarling and snapping its toothy jaws, it stood on top of the bunk.

Pihra. It had to be Pihra.

She had been the only other person in the room with me. Her empty robe lay on the floor.

They are Shape Shifters, Martan had told me.

Facing my two formidable opponents, I lifted my hands. "Okay, I give up."

The creature slipped off the bunk, stood on its hind legs and stared into my face. "Don't do that again!" she said, the voice a deep growl. "Next time we will rip you apart."

The outlines of her hairy body wavered, changed in front of my eyes. This time she took on human form. Her face looked human, but not her eyes.

She held out a hand. I put the weapon into it. "No hard feelings?" I said, grinning.

She didn't smile.

"What happened in here?"

I looked at Sehla, also in human form now, and naked. I didn't see any clothing on the floor, so I assumed she had been naked all along.

"Our guest tried to escape," Pihra said.

"Tsk, tsk," Sehla said and came closer. Displaying her fangs, she smiled at me. "Don't you enjoy our company? I was under the impression you liked coupling with us."

"Oh, I do," I said, "but I'm not excited about what it is costing me."

She laughed. "It's a fair bargain. We give you enjoyment, you give us a little blood and your semen." She looked at Pihra. "Shall we proceed?"

"There'll be no feeding or collecting," Pihra said. She watched me intently.

The adrenalin flow had not stopped inside my body. I was wound up like one of those spring-loaded crossbows we used when I was a kid. I needed to get out of here before they decided to eliminate the threat I might represent.

"He is not what he appears to be," Pihra said softly.

I saw the glowing weapon in her hand, which hung casually down her side, and it wasn't one of those pellet-throwers Commander Ryker had shown me.

I moved before she could lift her hand. My stiffened fingers drove into the soft flesh of her throat, cutting off her air-supply. Not waiting to see if I had killed her, I swung towards Sehla. She was already beginning to change, but she was still human enough for my attack on her to be effective. Twisting her head with all the strength I could muster, I let her collapse to the ground.

Then I was out of the door, racing across the room beside the *hospital,* down a narrow corridor.

I ripped open the door to my prison cell. Martan and the others lifted their heads when I stormed in. "Why in such a hurry, Griffin?" Martan asked.

"I'm getting you out of here...now, move!"

All three men looked at me with pity in their tired eyes. "It's no use, Griffin. Where would we go? There is no place to run to."

I grabbed my clothes from underneath my bunk, slipped into them. "I have friends outside. We'll protect you. Come on, let's go!"

None of them moved. I turned towards the door when I heard it being opened. One of our guards stepped through. I grabbed him by his horns, pulled him into the room and slammed him onto the metal floor. He kicked once, and then lay still.

Bending down, I pried the weapon from his fingers and gave it a quick examination. It had a trigger, like any other gun, also a black button at the top. I pushed the button. The gun began to glow in my hand.

Smiling grimly, I left our prison cell. As expected, another guard waited for me outside. Aiming for his chest, I shot him before he could bring up his own gun. The stench of burning flesh rose strong in the confinement of the corridor.

When I turned to run down the stairs at the end of the passageway, three of the Stardogs cut off my escape. Two more came down from the other side. They jumped back into a niche in the wall when they saw me.

"Give it up, Human," one of them called. "You'll never get out alive."

The three by the stairs had dropped flat. I couldn't see them, but I knew they were there. I could hear them breathing.

"We told you, Griffin," Perto said when I stepped back into the room. "They've got you trapped like a *Rock-hare* inside its cave."

I gave him a wolfish grin. "This *Rock-hare* has teeth and claws." I lifted my newly acquired weapon. Effective little toy. I'll burn them as they try to come into the room."

"I like your optimism, Griffin, but you're only fooling yourself. They'll just let us starve or die of thirst in here."

"We'll see," I said. I could hear them moving outside in the corridor. Then I heard loud shouts and the hissing of discharging lasers. Earth-made lasers. I knew, rescue was near. The crashing of falling bodies, confirmed my assumption. Then there came silence, except for the sound of heavy boots on the metal floor.

I lowered my gun when I saw the shadow of someone blocking the doorway. Then a stocky figure dressed in the metallic battle-gear of the Terran Empire entered the room.

"What took you so long, Kelsey?" I asked.

Kelsey scanned the room. I couldn't see his face behind the closed visor, but I knew him by the insignia on his chest and by the size of his body. He was the smallest member of our team.

"Are you alright, Major?" he asked, his voice amplified by the external speakers of the suit.

"I'm fine," I said and sat down on the bunk. Suddenly a terrible feeling of fatigue washed through me. "But I might need your assistance to get out of here," I added with a voice gone weak.

"We'll take care of you, Major. We have everything under control."

I heard others moving in the corridor. Probably Wu and Cherryh. Possibly even Meadow. I relaxed, and grinning weakly, I gave my three roommates the thumbs up. "The cavalry has arrived," I said, "you've been rescued."

Chapter Seventeen

Leaning heavily on Kelsey, I managed to climb down the stairs. The motionless bodies that lay in the corridor and on the stairs were neither human nor were they Yellowhorns. While dying they had reverted to their original shape.

"Ugly critters," Kelsey commented as we stepped over them.

Perto, who came behind us, gave one of the corpses a vicious kick, cursing loudly at the same time.

"There are some women upstairs," I said to Kelsey.

"We'll get you out of here first, Major." Kelsey growled. "Your safety is number one priority."

I grinned. "Whoever said that they've replaced your heart with an artificial one, was a liar," I said.

He just grunted. "Cherryh is keeping watch outside, but be alert. Some of the aliens took off in their vessel just before we arrived. They may be coming back."

"What about Killic? I think it would be a good time for him to make an appearance. With the skimmer."

"He's been contacted. He should arrive soon."

Kelsey was not one for long conversations. This was probably already too much talking for him.

Wu and Meadow stood by the entrance. Wu in his battle-uniform, but his visor up. He gave me a lopsided smile, his almond eyes tiny slits. "You're okay, Major?"

I nodded. "I'm fine."

Meadow gave me a concerned once-over. "You don't look fine," she said, almost accusing. "What happened?"

"Later!" I shrugged it off, even though I felt like crap. "I'll survive."

"Alright," she said, but didn't seem convinced. Watching the stairs behind us, she waited until Kelsey and I made our exit, then she followed us.

It was daylight outside, but I knew it was evening be the position of the red sun. The trees and houses threw long shadows across the dirt-packed street.

The street appeared empty, the alien vessel gone.

"What about the women in that house?" I asked Meadow.

"There is nothing we can do for them here," she said. "We'll have to transport them back to the facilities at headquarters where their pregnancies can be terminated without putting them in danger. None of them carries a human child."

"I know. I witnessed a birthing. It wasn't pretty."

"What went on in there, Major?" Cherryh asked as he approached us from the shadows of the houses. He looked at the black cone-shaped structure. His visor was up, like Wu's. I could see the hard lines on his dark face. "I saw those women," he said with a tight voice.

"The Stardogs are using them for breeding, but I believe we've stopped their little breeding program here. You can read the details in my report later. Right now we'll have to deal with the threat the natives represent." I leaned against Kelsey, who still held my arm. The strength seemed to ebb from my legs. I knew the problem, but I could do nothing about it right now.

The microcomputer inside me tried to analyze the substance Pihra and Sehla had introduced into my body, but failed to do so. I just knew that it had created havoc with my nervous system and caused the failure of some of my special implants.

It took a few moments until my system balanced itself while bypassing certain components, but it would be only temporary. I needed to get back to headquarters, where I could be hooked up to a more sophisticated medical unit.

Straightening up, I said, "Let's get going."

Before we managed to take more than a few steps, a flat, oval object came swooping across the treetops and circled the black alien structure. As it flew over it a second time, a bright flash spat from it, bathing the cone-shaped building with a fiery green light. The black walls began to bubble like a mountain of soap. It burst with a hissing sound, spewing black gob into the air.

Then the building collapsed and melted with the speed of a snowball doused with boiling water.

It all happened so quickly, and before any of us realized what had occurred, we were staring at a heap of melted shiny rubble.

Kelsey and Cherryh were the first ones to react. With a curse, both men lifted their laser rifles, tracked the alien vessel and almost simultaneously pulled the trigger.

Even though I had witnessed it many times, I could still appreciate the terrible power those weapons unleashed.

So silent.

So destructive.

So final.

The alien vessel exploded in the evening sky, showering us with a cloud of multicolored sparks.

As we silently walked back to camp, a group of Yellowhorns came galloping towards us. They halted their beasts when Kelsey burned a wide strip of grass in front of them. They didn't interfere when we entered one of the tents.

Cherryh and Wu stationed themselves outside, while Meadow told me to sit down onto one of the furs on the floor. Kelsey strapped a small, portable auto-doc around my left biceps. I took the skullcap from his hands and put it on myself.

The last thing I remember was the prick of a tiny needle.

* * * *

"How are you feeling?" Meadow watched as I wolfed down the big juicy steak she had prepared for me. Some of it was a little charred, but I didn't care. "Great," I said around a mouthful and washed it down with water from a small cup Kelsey had supplied from his pack.

"You had us worried, Major," he said beside me. He looked me over thoughtfully. "You must have lost a few pounds."

"A few," I agreed and grinned. I looked down at myself. "Damn it! I'm still naked. Is there no shame inside you?"

Kelsey grinned. "We've seen plenty of you, Major. Now is not the time to be self-conscious."

"How much do you remember?" Meadow asked.

I cringed and looked through the opening of the tent. I could see the spot where the alien structure had been standing. Now I saw nothing but melted twisted metal.

How much did I remember? That was the problem with the implanted artificial memory-chips. It was all there. Every bit of it and I could relive everything over and over again.

If I wanted to, I could wipe it all away, but I knew I had no choice. I had just too much vital information stored inside me. It needed to be reviewed, evaluated.

For the first time we made actual contact with the Stardogs. Intimate contact. Weaknesses could be found in the enemy that might be very important in other confrontations.

Too bad Pihra and Sehla were dead.

Thinking about them, I could feel a stirring between my legs. I knew it would take many days until my system flushed out every fragment of the drug-like substance I absorbed through my sexual encounters with Pihra and Sehla.

Until then I would be as horny as hell.

The auto-doc analyzed the foreign substance in my bloodstream and found the antidote: water, just plain water. I just needed to drink lots of it.

Wu stuck his head into the tent. His black, slanted eyes sparkled. "One of these clowns out here has been raving for the last couple of days about a challenge. He wants to tear apart the coward who is hiding behind women and metal men." He grinned. "That's us, Major. The coward, I assume, is you. I don't know what he means by women. I only see Meadow. Are you ready to talk to him?"

I grinned back. "I guess I am." I stood up and stretched.

"How about your uniform?" Kelsey asked.

"No." I shook my head. "Not yet."

Naked, I walked out of the tent. About fifty meters away, (53.75 meters, to be exact), Callawhan sat on his mount. A mass of warriors waited behind him, their Ginsa-staffs pointing in our direction.

"Fools," I murmured, "as if those sticks worried me."

"They're weapons," Kelsey, who walked beside me, said. "Take at least a blaster."

I shook my head. "I have to do it this way, Kelsey. Don't worry.'

He stayed behind as I walked on, but I heard the silent click as he unclipped his gun. I smiled. Kelsey was a good man, he had one fault...he was too damn efficient.

Callawhan dismounted as I stopped ten meters in front of him

"Dan Griffin," the Yellowhorn leader sneered, his left hand facing the sky. "I thought you crawled away with your tail between your legs." He looked at my semi-erect organ and laughed with a loud gurgling sound. "Do you come to fight or to copulate?"

I didn't laugh. "I came to talk, Callawhan."

"He came to talk!" Callawhan laughed, looking at the ring of grim warriors behind him. Some of them joined his merry laughter. His hand made an abrupt motion. "No talk!" he barked.

I pointed first at the empty burned spot to our left, then at the sky. "Better talk," I suggested. "You witnessed the easy destruction of your allies. The Terran Empire is mighty and invincible. We crush our enemies, but our friends are rewarded."

He looked at the rubble. I heard the uneasy shuffling of his warriors.

"The metal men are your friends?" Callawhan asked.

"I am their leader," I said.

A thoughtful look came into his yellow eyes. "You command these metal warriors? They fear you?"

"They don't fear me, Callawhan. They fear nothing, but they listen to me. If I give the command they would wipe out your whole army, kill every warrior before the sun reaches the highest point in the sky."

"If that is true, if you command such power, why would you want to talk with me, Dan Griffin?" Callawhan asked. I detected the sly note. "What do I have that you want? Maybe you fear me?"

"I don't fear you, Callawhan." I smiled. "But you are right, you have something valuable. You possess great leadership. You are a warrior with a vision, somewhat tainted vision, but it can be adjusted. With our help you could see your dream come true."

"What dream?"

"To unite the tribes, Great Wir, but to live in peace with the Terrans."

"Never!" shouted another voice. "Don't listen to him. We are many. They are only a few. We can defeat them."

Callawhan turned to look at the speaker. "Ah, Plactor, my impulsive nephew," he said. "Since when do you make decisions for me?"

Plactor stepped forward, his yellow eyes blazing. Addressing the warriors behind him, he called, "Callawhan is getting old and weak. I say we fight!" He turned and threw his Ginsa-staff at me.

I caught it in the air.

With a contemptuous snort, I broke it in half. Plactor roared and, swinging his kiso-blade, he attacked me.

It was time for a demonstration.

As he reached me I stepped aside, grabbed his knife-arm with my left, rammed my knee into his midriff and with my other hand I broke his neck.

He was dead before he hit the ground.

Callawhan's face showed no expression, only his yellow eyes widened for a moment. He looked at his dead nephew. "You killed him so easily," he said. "Without a weapon."

"No weapons are needed to kill," I said.

"So fast and with such ease." He looked at me. "How would you have killed me had I chosen to fight?"

"Just as easily," I replied.

"Let us talk."

* * * *

Kelsey stuck his head through the entrance to my tent. "One of the natives wants a word with you, Major."

"Alright." I slipped into my shirt and strapped on my laser, but just for show. Callawhan had promised me there would be no more bloodshed between his people and mine. Concessions were made on both sides, but we had agreed on a truce.

Kelsey pointed at a native standing a short distance away. "He claims he knows you."

I didn't recognize the young warrior. He was not a Yellowhorn. His clan-ring identified him as a warrior of the Stag-clan.

"I am Thorgas," he said, as he came close, touching his lips and his forehead. "Threehorn's brother."

I didn't show my surprise. Making the appropriate sign, I said, "I was Threehorn's blood-brother, but I guess you know."

He smiled and held out his right hand. Again, he took me by surprise. Shaking hands was not the custom of the tribes.

As I squeezed his hand, I remembered him. He had been just a child the last time I stayed with his clan. "You have grown, Thorgas. You're a warrior now. What can I do for you?"

"I wish to talk with you about Threehorn."

We sat and talked for a long time. We spoke of the old days, when Threehorn had been alive. It brought back many memories, talking about those carefree times. He wanted to know everything his brother and I had done, but when we talked about Threehorn's death, his yellow eyes darkened and the bristles on his head and neck stiffened.

"I know who killed my brother," he said, "and the killer has not been punished."

The surprise must have shown in my face. Even he saw it. "How do you know?" My voice sounded strange in my ears.

His eyes were still dark. Again, he made the truth-sign. "I was there, Dan Griffin. I watched as they murdered Threehorn and the human, my brother fought. I saw them put the knife into your hand, as you lay unconscious beside the other man."

Even though I had complete control over my body, I couldn't seem to still the trembling of my hands. "Who did it, Thorgas? How many were there, and would you recognize them again, after all these years?"

He made a sign, underlining his words. "There were three of them. I would recognize them anywhere. Their images are burned into my mind until I am dead." He looked silently at me for a time, as was the custom before an important statement was made. Then he said, "Your life may be in danger, Dan Griffin. One of the killers is sharing your food."

When he told me who, I was not greatly surprised, but I cursed silently as he described the other two, and I wowed to have justice done.

We touched elbows when we parted. He invited me to come and spend some time with him and his tribe. When I asked him about his sister, Blue Petal, he smiled and wriggled the little finger of his left hand. "She has never forgotten you, Dan Griffin, but she has taken a mate. His name is Kurbrak, which in your language means *Sky-climber*. He is a brave and wise warrior and a member of the tribal council. You would like him."

I watched him walk away. He walked proud, like his brother. Some day he would be part of the council. I never did ask him why he joined Callawhan's army.

Chapter Eighteen

"I can't agree with this preposterous treaty," Senator Humboldt shouted, his face red. "We can't just supply these savages with modern weapons!"

"I didn't promise them any *modern* weapons," I said, suppressing a smile. The Senator had no idea what classified as a *modern* weapon. "The only rifles we will sell them are bolt-action rifles with a magazine capable of holding a maximum of five bullets. No automatics or semi-automatics, no machine-guns, no lasers, or even handguns." I shrugged. "Unfortunately, thanks to some unscrupulous smugglers, they already possess an unknown number of all the weapons I mentioned. We just have to deal with that."

"We're not even allowed lasers on Redsky. Our status should be changed and we should be able to import weapons that are more modern. At least for our military. We need to be able to protect our citizens."

I looked at the speaker. He had changed since I saw him last, ten years ago, but I remembered him well. He didn't seem to remember me. Thirty pounds heavier, most of the weight around his middle, his face round and chubby, he didn't look as handsome as he used to. I never liked him. It didn't really surprise me that he made Senator. He had always been ambitious and ruthless, not to mention the fact that he was the son of Bertram Clarke, the Minister of Justice.

"I have given that some thought, Senator Clarke, and I will make recommendations that the military will be equipped with better weaponry, but I'm not sure if I want to include lasers."

"Why not?" He gave me a defiant look.

"Why not?" I repeated, stepping close to him. "I'll tell you why not, Senator Clarke. Because Redsky is a Class D planet. Does that answer your question?"

"Frankly, no, it does not." He glared at me. "Some small-minded bureaucrat with a God-complex somewhere in a glass tower office in the employ of the mighty Terran Empire decided to give our planet, a planet he's never seen, a classification that prohibits certain weapons, advanced means of transportation, the kind of power source we are allowed to use, and who knows what else. I think it's time to change things."

I chuckled. "Is that so? You think it's time to change things?" I leaned even closer. "You know, Robert, I'm surprised you didn't stumble over all these words, and all in one coherent sentence. You must have taken evening classes. Ten years ago, your brain would have exploded just thinking of these issues. However, it doesn't change anything. "

"What do you mean?"

"I mean you were an asshole then, and you still are an asshole."

"What?" He looked at me with indignation. "You have no right…Who the hell are you to even talk to me like that?"

He still didn't recognize me. We both had changed, except the weight I gained didn't increase the girth of my belly. When I spoke to him again, I dropped the stilted accent they spoke in the courts of the Terran Empire and used the common dialect of Redsky. "I am Major Daniel Griffin, Representative of the Terran Empire, and I decide the fate of your planet, Senator Clarke."

He stared at me, recognition dawning in his face. Then he shook his head and murmured, "This can't be."

"I didn't quite understand you," I said, switching back to the Terran accent.

"For a moment I thought you were someone I knew, but I must be wrong, even though there is a certain resemblance. I guess the name threw me. The man I thought of can't be alive anymore."

"You weren't wrong, Robert, old friend," I said, smiling. "I'm very much alive."

I registered the increase of his heartbeat, measured the tiny droplets of perspiration that appeared on his skin. "Impossible!" he blurted out. "You're toying with me, sir. You're just a look-alike. You don't even sound like him. Besides, he was a criminal."

"You know, Robert," I abandoned my phony accent for good, "I'm surprised that your good old friend Castor hasn't informed you of my presence here."

"Mayor Margin and I haven't been in contact for many years," he said.

"I wonder why. I thought you two were close friends."

"He is involved in things I'm not."

"Like what?"

"I'd rather not discuss." He eyed my shrewdly. "If you really are who you claim to be, then you haven't changed much. Still trying to stick your nose into things you should leave alone. Castor Margin is connected to powerful people you don't want to mess with. Just some friendly advice."

"You wouldn't by any chance be talking about that criminal organization that calls itself *The Winged Serpent*?" I spoke loud enough so everyone in the room could hear me. "Let *me* tell *you*, I am involved with people who are possibly a bit more powerful than that bunch of slavers and gun-runners."

His eyes grew wide as I spoke and he looked around the assembled senators, who had been following our conversation with some interest. "I want it to be known that I have nothing at all to do with *The Winged Serpent* and that I was not the one who implied that said organization is involved in criminal activities." He glared at me and lowered his voice. "You'd be smart to retract your statement. You never know who might be listening."

He sat down, sweating profusely.

"That was quite an informative conversation, Major Griffin, and a waste of our valuable time," Senator Humboldt commented sarcastically, "but I do agree with Senator Clarke. Our status should be upgraded, considering the threat we face from Isram. Those fanatics are ready to move against us, start a *Holy War*, and we are without the superior weapons they are rumored to possess."

"Rumors," I said mildly. "Do you have proof?"

"Not directly, but they've closed the border against anyone trying to enter their country. That should be proof enough of their plans." He pointed a finger at me. "What are you and the mighty Terran Empire going to do to protect us against a horde of bloodthirsty religious fanatics overrunning the rest of Redsky?"

"I am aware of the problem at the eastern border," I said. "Prime Minister DePratt doesn't think it *is* a problem. According to him, you could have handled it yourself. However, we have our own reasons to investigate the situation, so let me assure you, Senator Humboldt, we will make sure there is no war, holy or otherwise."

The Senator heaved a deep sigh. "I hope so."

"Senator Humboldt," I said, "I understand you represent Westland. Who is the Senator for Newland?" I pretended not to know.

"That would be Senator Clarke, sir."

"Ah, Senator Clarke." I turned back to my old friend, who sat in his chair, still sweating. "Tell me, Senator, who pulled the strings that made you Senator for Newland?"

He rose in his seat and shouted. "I protest against these kinds of remarks. If you must know...nobody pulled any strings. I have worked very hard to rise to this position."

"What did you do that was so hard?"

"I put in a lot of volunteer work in my community, for one thing. And..."

I lifted a hand. "Volunteer work, I like that. Have you ever put your life on the line for your country, Senator Clarke? Have you ever killed anyone?"

"I'm not a soldier," he said with indignation. "I was never put into the position where I had to kill someone. I'm not a murderer."

"I am a soldier," I said, looking into his eyes, "I have killed, but you don't have to be a soldier to kill someone. Even if you yourself never killed anyone, you could still be guilty of murder, just by association. Or neglect."

"Are you accusing me of anything?"

"No." I smiled. "Just trying to make a point." I looked at the other assembled Senators. "I am aware that there are problems with the native population. I am also aware that in Northland and in the province of Ariba there is a group of sportsmen who call themselves *Horn-hunters* who organize competitions to promote the *Acquisition of Trophies* and they pay huge rewards for the severed horns of a killed warrior." I made a sweeping motion with my finger. "Just knowing about it and doing nothing is as good as an admission of guilt. Maybe giving the native warriors better weapons will level the playing field a little."

"You don't mean that, I hope," Senator Barron rumbled. "We have enough tribes with modern weapons in Northland. We don't need any more." He glared at me from under bushy eyebrows. "And I resent your allegation, Major Griffin. I am not aware of any competitions by so-called *Horn-hunters.* This whole thing is preposterous." He sat down, flustered and angry.

"You are aware of it now, Senator Barron, and I recommend when you get back to Northland you begin investigating my *so-called* allegation." I spoke sharply, not because I wanted to enforce my suggestion, but because I knew he had to know about it, and I felt strongly connected to the tribes. My eyes fell on the man sitting beside Barron.

"Senator Granger, you haven't said anything so far. How are things in Ariba? Surely, you must have heard of the Horn-hunters. Your own brother is one of the members."

"My brother?" The Senator heaved his big body out of his chair. I didn't think a fat man like him could get up so fast. "That is a lie. My brother doesn't even know how to fire a rifle."

"I'm not talking about your little brother Astor. I'm talking about Gerald Tollmann, the president of Tollmann Enterprises, a company that sells sports equipment. You know, guns, ammunition, and other toys for real men. I am aware that he's only your half-brother, but still, he is a relative."

Granger shook his head in disbelief. "Where do you get all your information from?"

"You'd be surprised how much information can be gained just by talking to the right people." I chuckled. "Don't forget, I am not bound by any restrictions. I have the most sophisticated equipment at my disposal. Computers, spy-satellites. Tiny spybots that are smaller than an insect and even look like one. They can be attached to anything and anyone. I'm telling you this to give you an idea what you are dealing with, and a little something to ponder."

"Are you spying on us?" His already red face just took on another shade.

I shrugged. "I'll use any method available to me to find out what I need to know. Remember, I am the ultimate law enforcer on Redsky. I can do anything I want."

I left them sitting in their chairs. I registered their heartbeats, the amount of perspiration on their faces, and their increased breathing. Wu, who had quietly been listening in the back, gave me a small grin as he opened the door for me. His slanted eyes looked even smaller in his round face. "Weren't you a little hard on them, Major?" he asked when we walked down the corridor.

"Not even close, Wu," I said, but I returned his grin.

* * * *

Governor Delhouse was an old man...for Redsky.

"I'll be eighty-five next month," he told me, his thin, veined hands folded in front of him on the polished wooden desk. "They promised me a rejuv-treatment when my term is up." He leaned back in his chair. "That will be in six months. I hope I last that long."

"Why shouldn't you last, your Excellency?" I smiled. "You seem to be in good health."

Sighing, he stared at me over a pair of rimmed spectacles, something one didn't see on most civilized planets. People usually wore artificial contact lenses, either permanently attached to their eyes or, in many cases, temporary lenses, which could be exchanged at will with lenses of different colors. Of course, he wouldn't need either after his rejuv-treatment.

"It's not my health I'm worried about, Major. You know the problem we have at the eastern border. It could flare up any day and I wish I weren't here to deal with it."

"I fixed one of your problems already. Maybe I can do something about this one," I suggested.

"These are not unorganized savages with spears and knifes, Major. We're dealing here with five million religious fanatics. All of them potentials soldiers with modern weapons."

He saw me smile and lifted his hands. "No energy-weapons, of course, but machine guns, grenades, small canons." His bushy eyebrows pulled together. "It is not entirely true, though, when I said no energy-weapons. Apparently, somebody is smuggling weapons to Redsky. There are rumors that lasers are among them."

"I know," I said, remembering the laser I had taken from the thug I'd shot. "By the way, I would not call the natives 'savages' with spears and knifes. They have projectile weapons, and they know how to handle them. They will have more. I made a deal with Callawhan and I plan to keep that promise."

"Do you really think it is wise or even right, to sell those types of weapons to the natives?"

"It is not a question of right or wrong, your Excellency. They have plenty of them already, thanks to the Stardogs and the smugglers. Maybe this way we can control the kind of weapons they can buy."

"I don't know, Major." The Governor shook his grizzled head. "Twenty years ago, when I took this post, Redsky was a quiet place, but so much has happened these last five years." He paused to light a small pipe, slowly and carefully, taking his time. Puffing vigorously, he stared at the clouds of smoke. "These Stardogs...what are they like?"

I shrugged. "We don't know much about them, even now. The last report we had described them as dog-like creatures with three fingers and a long, opposing thumb."

"They are not like that, I gather?"

"Not at all." The voluptuous images of Pihra and Sehla popped into my mind and a soft pounding in my loins brought a tinge of loss and sadness. "They represent a great danger, your Excellency," I said. "They are Shape Shifters who are able to mimic human beings to perfection. They most likely possess other, more dangerous and frightening abilities, which we don't know about. I managed to gain access to one of their bases. I stayed there only for a short time and almost fell victim to their experiments."

He raised a questioning eyebrow. "Experiments?"

"They are using human women as breeders for their offspring and human men as sperm-donors."

"They copulate with humans?"

"It seems that way. I will get you access to my report, after it has been evaluated."

The aroma of his tobacco hung heavy in the small room, irritating my sensitive nose. Time to finish our conference. "With your approval, your Excellency, I will visit the Holy Temple in Rhandistan and request audience with the Grand Minister of Isram and with their Thalmani."

I asked for his approval only out of courtesy. I could put this planet under Martial Law any time I felt it necessary...and he knew it. Even though he symbolized the might of the Terran Empire on Redsky, I outranked him, since I represented the military power of the Empire.

He nodded within his cloud of smoke. "Do what is necessary, Major Griffin. I don't really care, as long as it results in a peaceful settlement of this problem."

When I shook his hand, I wondered briefly whose tail he stepped on twenty years ago to have ended up on a backwater dead-end planet like Redsky. Why he took up residence in Fort Locust was also a question I asked myself. He could have lived in one of the luxurious suites in the residential area of the Spaceport in more civilized surroundings. His position as Governor entitled him, but he probably had his reasons why he chose to live in the Spartan conditions of a military compound.

Kelsey waited for me outside, beside the skimmer. "Everything alright, Major?" he asked.

I nodded, suppressing a smile. Ever since he rescued me from the clutches of the Stardogs, he hovered around me like a mother hen. He had been with me on *Custer*. Together we watched Marco Bandini die, the victim of a beautiful, but deadly plant-woman. It left scars on us, more so on Kelsey than on me.

He hadn't cared much for women before, now he mistrusted them completely. We never really touched on the subject, but as far as I knew, he wasn't a homosexual. His need for sex was probably not very great.

"Take me back to the hotel in Old Town. Maybe tomorrow we'll go back to headquarters. I'm due for a debriefing session with DIDA. Apparently my report was not comprehensive enough."

"We've all been debriefed once already," Kelsey said.

I smiled. "Not the way I will be, trust me."

* * * *

There was a message from Meadow at the hotel desk for me.

Took a little trip with Darl. He wants to show me a few things. See you tomorrow night. Love. Meadow.

I shrugged and went up to my room. I had hoped to spend some time alone with her, but I guess she had other plans. I could imagine what Darl wanted to show her. *Not my business*, I thought.

I was just about to go and order some food, when I heard a soft knock on my door. Wondering who it could be, I went to open it.

She stood in the doorway, looking lost and a little scared, and as beautiful as the day I married her.

"Hi, Dan," she said with a small voice.

"Lane," was all I could say before she fell into my arms, sobbing uncontrollably. Holding her tight, I kissed the tears from her eyelids and her cheeks, not daring to kiss her lips. "Why did you come?" I whispered.

"Because I love you, damn you!" she cried out. "Why did you have to come back? My life was finally back to normal."

"You were lucky," I said bitterly. "Mine hasn't been normal ever since the day they found me lying beside Garth."

Her mouth searched mine. I kissed her sweet lips, stroked her beautiful hair, and inhaled her fragrance. "Lane, Lane, my lovely Lane," I moaned. "Why did this have to happen to us?"

She molded her soft body against mine. I felt my hardening organ pressing into her belly. Giggling, she wriggled her hips. "You haven't changed much," she whispered, her breath suddenly catching in her throat.

Sweeping her off her feet, I carried her into the bedroom. We fell on top of the bed and I ripped my shirt off my upper body. Pushing my pants past my hips, I moved between her parting thighs. I didn't give her a chance to take off her panties. I just pushed one leg-opening aside and slid my rigid mast into her dripping pussy.

"You haven't changed, either," I groaned as I moved inside her burning sheath. "Still hot and soaking wet."

She gasped and moved against me. "It's been a long time since I felt like this," she sobbed and cried out when an orgasm shook her body. "Oh, Dan, I've missed you so much. I've missed this so much."

For a little while, it seemed as if we had never been apart. The ten years I had been gone, fell away like a bad dream. For a little while, we were two young lovers who couldn't get enough of each other. We were lost in a world of lust, love, and passion.

But only for a little while.

When I came inside her, she clung to me, whimpering, riding the crest of her own orgasm. I didn't pull out of her, just held her tight and lay there, cradled by her warm thighs and loving arms.

"I love you, Dan," she whispered softly. "I love you like I never loved another man."

"Not even Castor?" I asked, breaking the spell that had been holding us captive.

"Not even Castor," she murmured and sighed.

Her legs fell open as she released me and I pulled out of her warm sheath, rolled onto my back beside her. Looking up at the ceiling, reality catapulted me back to the present. I became acutely aware of my heartbeat, of her heartbeat, of the perspiration on her skin, of the amount of fluid I had pumped into her.

Damn those gadgets inside my body!

Whom did I try to fool? I was not the same man of ten years ago. It wasn't only time that separated us. We could never go back to the way it had been.

"What are you thinking, Daniel?" She stroked my chest with soft fingers. I measured her elevated pulse, 96 beats per minute. My own back to 72, normal for me. That little computer inside my chest made sure of that.

I turned my head and smiled at her. "Nothing right now," I said. "Just enjoying the moment."

She snuggled against me. "So am I. I wish we could turn back the clock ten years and make everything that's happened go away."

"I wish that too," I said, "but I'm afraid, that wish won't come true. Fate has dealt us a bad hand, sweetheart, and we have to make the best of it." I watched a tear roll onto her cheek and wiped it away with my finger.

"We do, don't we." She smiled sadly. "You never asked me how old Kelly was."

"You really didn't give me a chance."

"She turned ten just a few days ago. She was born eight months after they arrested you."

"She's small for her age," was all I could say.

"She's your daughter, Daniel."

That damn gadget behind my breastbone kept my heart beating at exactly 72 beats per minute, dampened the flow of adrenaline and kept me from jumping up to smash my fist into the wall, but it couldn't keep away the icy hand that wanted to pull my heart out of my chest.

Kelly, my sweet little daughter, who called another man 'daddy'. A man whose guts I hated with a passion.

"And Castor married you, even though you had a child from me?" I asked, bewildered.

"He loves her, you may not believe that."

"Castor never loved anyone in his life."

"He loves *me*," she said softly.

I pushed her hand away and sat up. "And you? Do you love him?"

"Not the way I love you, Dan. I told you that already." She reached out to touch my shoulder. "Nobody can ever take your place in my heart." She pulled her dress over her head and slipped out of her panties. "Take off your pants and boots and make love to me again," she said gently. "I want to feel you on my bare skin."

She looked so beautiful, sitting naked in my bed, her long black hair spilling across her shoulders, partially covering her lovely breasts.

When I slid on top of her again, she closed her legs. "Take it slow this time, my darling. Touch my body the way you used to, make my skin tingle and my vessel quiver with anticipation, before you penetrate my flower and possess my body and soul."

Oh Lane, sweet Lane. It used to turn me on when you talked like that, but somehow the magic is gone. Now these words sound empty, stilted.

I've lost more than my good name and my freedom ten years ago. Much more.

Kissing her full lips, I ran my hands over her beautiful body, touched her breasts, her flat belly. My mouth moved to her neck, to her breasts, found one of her nipples and fastened upon it. She moaned and opened her legs. Her hand curled around my stiff member, stroked it gently.

"Take me now, my sweet love," she whispered, "fill me up with your hot piece of flesh, and make me delirious with pleasure."

I let her guide me into her burning sheath, slid easily into her. She whimpered and raked my back with her fingers. "It's just you and I now, my love, don't think about anything or anyone else. Pretend we never lost our innocence."

It was easy to forget in her arms. Her great passion made me feel relaxed and happy, and she made me feel wanted and loved.

"Lane, my darling Lane," I groaned, giving in to her coaxing and whisperings of love. It was easy to pretend in her arms. "I will always love you, no matter what," I told her.

"Promise?" She slammed her taut belly against mine, a soft moan escaping her half-open lips. "You make me feel so good, Daniel," she sobbed. "Oh Daniel…now…NOW!"

* * * *

Next morning I awoke early. Lane still slept. I watched her as she lay beside me, her long black hair framing her oval face, her full lips curled up into a satisfied smile.

Some women are beautiful only after applying make-up to their faces. Lane looked as lovely in the morning as she did when we went to bed. Few women are blessed with such natural beauty.

She sighed softly and turned, burying her face in the pillow.

Silently, I slipped out of bed and stepped into the shower cubicle. As the warm water streamed down my body, I became aware of a gnawing feeling in my stomach. I smiled, realizing we never did eat the night before. After drying off I ordered a hearty breakfast, then I tiptoed back into the bedroom.

Lane sat up and looked at me with sleepy eyes. "Dan." She smiled and yawned. "What are you doing out of bed?"

I laughed, enjoying the view of her lovely bare breasts above the blanket. "It is morning, sleepy. Get up. I ordered breakfast."

She yawned deeply and held out her arms. "Come and get me, I'm still too tired to move." She giggled when I pulled away the blanked, exposing her voluptuous naked body. She put one hand over her pubic area, the other across her breasts. "You are so bold, sir. I am an innocent maiden."

She loved to play games like that. It brought spice and excitement to our love life. Laughing, I lifted her out of bed. "You could have fooled me last night, young lady. My knees are still wobbly."

Her arms went around my neck, and nibbling on my ear, she whispered, "Why not come back to bed and rest your knees?"

I carried her into the shower and disengaged myself from her embrace. "First we'll have breakfast. My stomach is already crying for attention."

Laughing softly, she reached down and curled her fingers around my semi-erect organ. "So is this guy."

I moaned as she knelt in front of me. With a wicket glint in her eyes, she closed her full lips over the tip of my swollen member. Closing my eyes, I grabbed her thick black hair and gave in to the delicious feeling of her tongue flicking across the tip of my organ.

I opened my eyes when her mouth suddenly freed my pulsing mast. She slid up against me, her face flushed. "I don't know what's come over me, Dan. I've never done this before."

I smiled, kissing her gently. "It is alright, love," I said, turning her to face the mirror. "Bend down!" I commanded softly. She obeyed, leaning against the washbasin, her rump facing me. Gently, I spread her legs with my hand. The fleshy lips of her womanhood glowed pink below her smooth buttocks. She trembled as my organ touched them. I entered the slippery orifice and, with a cry, she pushed back against me, steadying herself on the basin.

Our eyes locked in the mirror. I took her slow and easy, holding her tight when her hips began to buck between my hands. Her dark eyes glazed over a few times, as she clutched me inside her, her face taking on a pained expression, but I knew she didn't suffer pain. When we finally cried out simultaneously, she stood still, her body frozen, only the hot walls of her sex-sheath pulsing with life, clutching frantically, her buttocks trembling in my groin.

After I pulled out of her, she rested her head on her folded arms for a while, and then she lifted her head to look at me in the mirror. "This is insane, Daniel," she said softly, but she smiled. She straightened and came into my arms. "You said you ordered breakfast. I think I really need it now."

"Me too," I said, chuckling, and watched her step gracefully into the shower-cubicle. "You are still so beautiful," I called as she turned on the water, "and I love you."

"I love you too," she called back, "but not until after breakfast."

Someone knocked on the outer door. I quickly slipped into a robe and went to open up. The maid walked in with our breakfast.

She smiled and put the tray on the table. "Is there anything else, sir?"

I chuckled. "There might have been...if I were alone."

She blushed and laughed good-humoredly, knowing that I was only half-kidding. I watched her swaying hips as she walked towards the door. She turned, giving me a long look out of dark, smoldering eyes. Her cheeks flushed. She smiled and said softly, "Maybe another time."

She closed the door quickly. I heard the sound of her footsteps, as she walked down the hall.

"Maybe," I murmured and turned as Lane walked into the room.

"This is all I could find in the closet." She giggled, pulling the thin, semi-transparent robe tightly around her. Her nipples stood out sharply and the dark areolae of her breasts were clearly visible behind the thin material. She looked delicious and I almost skipped breakfast. Sometimes a partially dressed woman looks sexier and more desirable than a completely nude one.

She noticed the hungry look in my eyes.

"Somehow I had a feeling this wasn't the right thing to wear if I wanted breakfast." She smiled. "I'm sorry, Daniel, but I really am hungry. My stomach is all queasy." She looked at me from behind lowered lashes. "Are you always this horny or is it just me?"

I knew it wasn't only her appearance that made me want her but those damn drugs the Stardogs injected into my system. Even the minute amounts, which must still be in my body, were powerful enough to trigger this reaction whenever I saw an attractive woman. Of course, I couldn't tell her that. "It's you, sweetheart, just you."

I sat down and watched her as she started to eat. Even though her memory had haunted me all these years, I had forgotten how beautiful she really was. Now, ten years older, she looked more mature, but more beautiful than ever. Tall, slim, full-breasted, her waist still as tiny as when we married. An artist's inspiration. And she had been mine. Now she belonged to someone else. A bitter hatred against the people who did this to me welled up inside me.

As quickly as these feelings came that's how quickly I dampened them. I couldn't afford to let them cloud my mind. Revenge was not the reason I had been sent here. There were bigger issues at stake, my own issues were not important.

Hell they weren't!

I emptied my glass of juice. It left a bitter taste in my mouth.

"You look angry." Lane studied my face. Then she reached across the table and stroked my cheek. "Did I do something to make you feel this way?"

I smiled at her. "Whatever you did, it wasn't your fault, Sweetheart. Sometimes, when we think everything is fine and nothing can go wrong, Lady Fate has a habit of surprising us."

Her expression turned suddenly sad. "You have changed, Daniel. A lot. Words like this would have never come out of your mouth before all this. I'm sorry I didn't stand by you when you needed me most." There were tears in her eyes. They slowly trickled down her cheek.

"So am I, but I'm not blaming you. We can't change what happened. We can only try to make things right."

Her tears were flowing freely now. "I don't know how, Darling. I am married to a man who has a lot of power and connections. I know he keeps secrets from me, and I don't pry into his affairs. Some of the people he associates with, they are not...nice." She stared at her plate. "He scares me sometimes."

"Do you feel you are in any danger? Has he ever threatened you? Hurt you?"

"No, nothing like that." She looked up, her eyes moist. "He loves me, but not like you. His love is...possessive. I belong to him."

"Nobody belongs to anyone." I spoke fiercely. "Nobody!"

"Oh, Daniel." She stood up and reached for my hand.

Without speaking, we walked back into the bedroom. She slipped out of her robe and lay down on the bed, naked and lovely. I stared at the dark triangle between her smooth thighs and, swallowing a lump in my throat, tried to control the pounding in my loins, but I felt only lust now. *I am not an animal,* I told myself, *I feel more for her than just pure lust. She was my wife. Still is...even if she is legally married to another man.*

It didn't help. With a feral shout I, fell between her widespread legs, frantically searching, until she whispered, "Easy, love, easy."

She guided me with a gentle hand and cried out when I entered her hot, dripping sheath. Passion overtook us both, but after awhile we slowed down and our lovemaking became tender and sweet. We spoke no more until the last moment, when she cried out, "Daniel…oh…Daniel!"

Then we lay exhausted in each other's arms. I felt happy and sad at the same time. There was no need to fool myself. Things could and would never be the same between us. We both changed and I had no legal claim on her. She was married to Castor Margin and he would not give her up without a fight. Many people could get hurt in the process.

"I should go," she said with a low voice.

I nodded and kissed her one last time. "Take care, my Darling."

Chapter Nineteen

After Lane left I ordered another breakfast. Steak and eggs, a pot full of coffee and a bottle of wine. I don't usually drink alcohol until noon, but today I would make an exception. I started my second glass of wine, when Kelsey knocked on my door. As softly as he had moved, my built-in sensor system had heard and recognized his footsteps.

When I opened up to let him in, he looked at me with a worried expression. "You didn't call us. Everything alright, Major?"

"Yes," I said. "Why shouldn't it be?"

"Is Meadow with you?"

"No, she left a message yesterday saying that she was going to spend the night with my old friend Darl Mitas. Won't be back until tonight."

Kelsey lifted an eyebrow and looked around, noticed the extra set of dishes on the table. "You had company?"

"My wife...ex-wife. She came for a visit."

"I see. Any objections if I sit down, Major?"

"Go ahead. A glass of wine?"

He lifted a hand. "Thank, you, no. You know better than to ask me that, Major."

I grinned. "You'll have to relax a little, Kelsey. Do you ever do anything for fun?"

"Not much." He sat down at the table. "I wouldn't mind some breakfast, though. I was actually just going to join the others downstairs."

"I'll order some. Help yourself to the fruit. It is fresh."

About to sit down again, I heard heavy footsteps outside in the hall. Kelsey looked up. "That's Killic," he said, stuffing a piece of fruit into his mouth.

Killic knocked and walked in. "I just finished talking to Chief

135

Hersch. He and his technicians have discovered an interesting thing on the surveillance net. He thought you might want to have a look at it."

"That's all he said?" I asked.

"That's all, but he sounded anxious." Killic planted his bulk into an empty chair and reached for the coffee pot. "Mind if I have a cup?"

"Have one. I better call for some more. Didn't expect guests for breakfast."

He grinned. "How about last night? Didn't you have a visitor?"

"Seems a man can't have any secrets around here."

"It's our job to protect you, Major," Kelsey said, munching on the last piece of toast. "You cannot afford to have secrets from us."

I shrugged. "Sometimes I still feel like a prisoner."

"We are soldiers of the Terran Empire, Major. In a sense, we are prisoners. There is a war going on, we have no choice but to fight. To keep human space free, we must give up our own freedom," Kelsey said with a solemn voice.

Killic laughed and applauded. "Well spoken, Kelsey. You've always had a flare for the dramatic." He emptied his mug and put it down hard. "But cut the crap in front of the Major. This fucking planet has not been kind to him."

Kelsey looked at me. "No offence, Major. I just got carried away a little."

"None taken, my friend." I smiled. "You are right, we have no choice."

"There is always a choice," Killic cut in. "At least we can always make the best out of any situation."

Kelsey grinned at him. "I guess you've been following your own advice. Haven't seen much of you these last couple of days. Been busy?" He turned to me. "Killic's taken a fancy to one of the girls."

"Oh?" I said, not really surprised. Killic had always been a woman-chaser.

"She's really cute, Major." Killic said with a grin. "Petite, young, great body, black silky hair, nice…"

"We get the picture, Killic," Kelsey interrupted him. "Spare us the boring details of your love life."

"What's her name?" I asked.

"Her name is Ninca," Killic said, a smug smile on his face.

"Well, I'm glad you're having a little bit of fun, unlike Kelsey, who doesn't believe in fun," I said. "By the way, we'll have to do something about those girls."

"They have nowhere to go." Killic had a thoughtful look on his face. "They are strangers in this town. Ninca tells me she's been a slave for over a year now. Some of the others even longer. She has been lucky, because her past master was an old man who only liked to look at her. A few of the other girls were literal love-slaves. We can't send them back to that life!"

"I know," I said. "They can stay here until we get back from Isram, then we'll see. We better get on our way now back to Headquarters. Call Wu and Cherryh."

Kelsey simply punched their codes into his wrist-comm. "Wu, Cherryh. Major wants to see you in his suite. On the double!"

I could have done that myself, but Kelsey liked to give orders. There wasn't really much that he enjoyed anymore. As my second-in-command, the others obeyed his orders without questions.

Wu and Cherryh arrived exactly three minutes later, both dressed in their uniforms. Cherryh had thrown a cloak over his wide shoulders. He was tall, well built, not quite as large as Killic and me, but still an imposing figure. Wu was even shorter than Kelsey, barely 160 cm tall, but stocky, nearly fat. Compared to him, Kelsey looked almost fragile.

But like Kelsey, like all of us, he was a rebuilt man. Strong. Fast. Dangerous.

His black slanted eyes glinted cold in a round, smiling face. Many an opponent had been fooled by his soft-looking, friendly appearance. Had they but only looked into his eyes!

"Morning, Major," he said, giving Killic and Kelsey a nod. "What's up?"

* * * *

Two hours later our skimmer landed beside the Administration building of the spaceport. Chief Hersch met us in his office. We followed him into the Security Center. He and his technical personnel had installed a new tracking device, one capable of detecting and identifying spacecraft entering the system the moment they materialized out of sub-space.

Hersch gave us a thin smile, as he proudly displayed the computer-enhanced picture on the giant screen. "We found it hiding on the smaller satellite. It's big, Major Griffin," he said, looking at me.

I stared at the huge alien ship.

"How long has that thing been sitting there?" Kelsey asked.

Hersch shrugged. "I don't know. Probably for quite some time. We only finished setting up three days ago."

"How did you discover it?" I asked.

"We launched a couple of drones. One is orbiting at two-hundred thousand km and the other one at three-hundred twenty-five thousand km, just a smidgen past the small moon's orbit."

"What exactly are we looking at?" Wu looked at the Chief and then at me.

"Definitely alien," Hersch answered. "Nothing like it in the memory banks."

"The Stardogs," Wu said. "I wonder what they're up to."

I wondered about the same thing.

* * * *

This time there was no field of flowers. The sky looked different, too. Tall, purple plants grew all around me and the air was humid and warm. Through openings in the roof of the alien plants, I caught glimpses of a reddish sky, dotted with bright white clouds.

I remembered this place. I had been there only a short time, searching for a missing scientist. It looked like a peaceful place...on the surface. Giant reptiles and other scaly denizens of the jungle made it dangerous and unpleasant.

I swung around when I heard movement behind me. Instead of facing a hungry carnivore, I stared at the lovely vision of a woman coming towards me.

"Angel?" I said.

She smiled. "You can relax, Daniel. There is no danger here." She wore flowers in her long dark hair. A white flower covered each nipple of her rounded breasts and her genital area. She came closer and took my hand. "Come, I will show you the little paradise I've created just for you."

She led me down a narrow path. We stopped beside a pond. I looked at the gently rippling water. It was so clear I could see colorful fish swimming below the surface. On the other side of the pond stood a small flock of large, red-winged birds with slender long beaks. They dipped them into the water to pick up tiny, wiggling creatures.

"You like it?" she asked.

I laughed. "What's there not to like. But I know this is not real."

"What is reality?" She sank to her knees and lay down on top of a mat made from soft reeds. Opening her arms, she said, "Come, relax in my arms."

I stretched out beside her, and then moved into her inviting embrace. Her breasts felt soft against my naked chest. Only now, I became aware of my nudity.

She kissed me gently and moved her hand down to my belly. When her fingers curled around my member, I reacted almost immediately. Laughing, she opened her satiny thighs and wrapped long legs around my torso. She was moist and warm when I slid into her gently clutching sheath. "Doesn't this feel real to you?" she whispered into my ear.

I moved in the embrace of her strong legs, pushed deep into her with powerful thrusts. She rotated her pelvis underneath me, milked my throbbing member with her pulsing softness.

Time seemed to slow down. Nothing else existed but the spot where we were joined. Waves and waves of pleasure washed through my body, taking away all the pain and bad memories that were cluttering up my mind. Healing and cleansing mind and body, repairing damaged organic and synthetic electrical circuits, reprogramming corrupt components, installing new programs and directives.

When I thought I had reached the peak of possible pleasure, a powerful orgasm gripped me. An orgasm so violent, it flung me into a dark void that seemed to go on forever. I was a god and the universe my mistress. Together we created world upon world, populated them with teeming life.

Then Eternity ended.

When I opened my eyes, I looked into the face of Licia, Professor Goldblat's assistant.

"Everything alright, Major?" she asked, smiling.

"Don't know yet," I said, looking down at myself. I was strapped onto a narrow bed, small pads with wires attached to them covering my naked body. Memory rushed back into my system.

I had just been through a debriefing.

They had changed a few things since my last 'joining' with D.I.D.A. The shiny cube with the blinking lights was gone. Instead, I looked at a shimmering wall full of pulsating colors and one huge screen its center. The wires, which were hooked up to my body, ran into the base of the bed I lay on.

"Hello, Daniel," a familiar voice came over hidden speakers.

"Hello, Angel," I said. "You look different."

Silvery laughter rang from the speakers. "Only on the outside. Maybe some day I will change that even more. Who knows, I might yet take on human form."

"Are you happy with what you found inside my brain?"

"Happiness means nothing to me, but I am satisfied with our progress. Your progress. You've given me much information to evaluate. Very important information. Take care, Major Griffin."

"You, too, Angel."

Chapter Twenty

When we got back to the hotel, the desk clerk handed me a sealed envelope, addressed to *Major Griffin* and marked *Urgent.* He shrugged when I asked who had given it to him.

"Just some kid," he said and went back to reading his magazine.

I smiled when I glimpsed pictures of nude girls. This guy would flip if he'd ever visit Earth or the other more advanced planets. Nobody there would be turned on by mere pictures. It had to be life-size holograms that moved and talked. With the right hook-ups, one could even have sexual intercourse or any perversion imaginable, with the lifelike projections, be it human, animal, or alien. The limits were set only by one's imagination.

Back in my room, I opened the envelope. It held a note and a photograph. I didn't have to guess what the note said. I read it anyway.

Major Griffin! If you want your girlfriends to live, you will leave Redsky within 24 hours. Don't look for them, or they will die. You will never see them again, but if you leave, they will live.

Grimly, I looked at the pictures of Meadow and Aleethy. Both of them were naked, their hands tied and a collar around their necks.

Slaves!

Somebody would pay for this, and I had a hunch who it would be!

Five minutes later Killic knocked on my door. He looked grim as he walked in. "Ninca is gone." His voice gave me the shivers.

"Just Ninca?" I asked.

He shook his head. "No, all the girls. I don't like it, Major. Something is wrong."

I handed him the picture and the note. He only needed one glance before he gave it back to me. "Who did it?"

He had automatically scanned the picture and note for fingerprints, just as I had done, but he lacked the information I had in my memory-web. "A recent companion of mine," I answered. "Lt. Niels DePratt. I know he is involved in this. But he's slippery and he has powerful accomplices."

"He's not as smart as he thinks. Already he's made one mistake," the blond man said matter-of-factly. "We'll get them back, Major."

"He made more than one mistake, Killic," I said. "His biggest one eleven years ago. I owe him."

He waited for an explanation and I gave it to him. "He murdered the best friend I ever had. His name was Threehorn and we were closer than brothers. Then he set me up for the murder of my brother-in-law. I lost my wife, my freedom, everything I held dear. I lost myself." I didn't hide the bitterness in my voice, not in front of Killic. At one time or another, we all felt the same way.

They had tampered with our bodies, but they had not dared tamper with our minds. Our minds set us apart from an emotionless machine...a robot.

Healthy bodies develop healthy minds was true only to a certain degree. They didn't take away the loneliness, the hatred and the thoughts of revenge embedded deeply in the dark recesses of our minds.

With a coded thought impulse we could suppress all emotions and become cold, efficient organic machines. However, the emotions were still there, waiting like coiled serpents to be released.

"We'll get him!" Killic said, his voice as cold as his blue eyes. "I'll crush him like a bug." His big fist closed as he lifted his hand. "Just like a bug...and he better not have hurt that lovely little girl!"

After I'd called the others, they came immediately to my room. I explained the situation to them and they all agreed with my decision not to leave Redsky. There is no way we would be intimidated by criminals or give in to their demands. I was quite certain they were bluffing when they threatened to kill the girls, but we couldn't take a chance.

I needed to talk to Darl Mitas and I cursed the lack of electronic communication devices on this planet. I never really realized how backwards Redsky was until now. The transportation system was lousy. Most people used horses and buggies. There were some airsleds around, but they were ancient and power packs were hard to come by.

The police department was better equipped, of course. They even had communicators, voice only, though. I couldn't contact Darl directly, so I had to find him through a dispatcher.

Cherryh was the only one with the multi-band transmitter on his belt. "Get me Police Headquarters," I instructed him. It took a couple of minutes until we got an answer.

The pleasant female voice, which seemed to originate somewhere in the middle of the room, sounded puzzled at first and even a little scared.

I couldn't blame her. Cherryh had literally blanked out all other calls and forced his own impulses over all the others. His voice must have sounded like the *Angel of Doom* in the woman's receiver.

"Who are you and what are you doing on police-frequency?" the voice asked with a slight tremor, but trying to sound authoritative.

"This is Major Griffin of the Terran Interplanetary Space Force," I said into the air. "I'd like to leave a message for Sergeant Mitas. Tell him I must talk with him immediately. In my hotel room. I am leaving Redsky within 24 hours."

After a moment of silence the woman answered, her voice still shaky. "I will tell him, Major Griffin."

Cherryh broke the connection and looked at me. "A bluff?" he asked.

I nodded. "Let them feel smug and secure in their false belief. The surprise will be so much greater." I even managed to smile.

From the desk clerk, we found out that two policemen had picked up Ninca and the other girls. He grinned. "Apparently, they are suspected of soliciting. Too bad, I didn't know that earlier."

Killic reached over the counter with one hand and grabbed the little guy's belt. Then he lifted him high into the air. "One more remark like that and you'll be wallpaper," the big man growled.

"Let him down," I said softly, "before he comes in his pants. You've probably given him the biggest thrill of his life."

Killic sat him down. Not too gently. "Go back to reading your filthy magazines, *scummer*," he said. "That's probably all you're capable of, anyway."

"What is going on here?" a familiar voice asked from the door. Darl looked at the cringing clerk, then at me.

"These men are assaulting me, Officer." The little man pointed a shaky finger at Killic. "Arrest this man."

"Shut up!" Killic glared at him.

"What the hell is going on, Dan?" Darl ignored the clerk. "I get this urgent message from the desk-sergeant to meet you. Then on my way here, I suddenly get another call from my superior, canceling the call. I was needed elsewhere. A more pressing situation had developed. I ignored that, smelling a rat. Can you explain?"

"Not here," I said. "Come to my suite."

My men were watching Mitas as he sat down. They didn't trust him.

"Where is Meadow?" I asked.

He looked surprised. "I have no idea. She is not with you?"

"No. Explain what happened!"

He stared at me, at the others. "What the hell is this?" he cursed. "Am I on trial here for something?"

"Meadow is missing, along with Aleethy and all of the other girls," I said calmly. "Meadow was with you last. I have her message, I also have a witness."

"You may have her message, but your facts are wrong, friend." He glowered at me. "She promised me a couple of exciting days. And then she takes off with that son-of-a-bitch DePratt! I never liked him."

"I am not accusing you of anything, Darl. I just want to find Meadow. Why did she go with DePratt? What made her change her mind?"

He sighed and shrugged. "I guess it's not her fault. I was just angry. We had just left the hotel, when Lt. DePratt and a couple of officers, friends of his, pull up and they tell me I was to go on a special shift. So DePratt offers to look after Meadow, that's all. I never thought anything of it." He looked around, uncomfortable. "It's the truth, I swear."

I nodded at Killic, who was still staring at him. "He doesn't know anything."

"Not about Meadow," Kelsey said, "but he hides something."

Again, I nodded. Although Darl's heartbeat was rapid, his voice strained, and he was perspiring profusely, he was telling the truth. "He has his suspicions, but nothing concrete." I turned back to Mitas. "Tell me about crooked cops," I said. "I'd like to hear something about the two friends of Lt. Niels DePratt. And tell me about Major Margin."

His head came up and his mouth opened, then closed. "He's powerful, Dan," he said after a while. "And he's got friends…influential friends."

"Yeah," I said. "So he has, but I'm not one of them."

"He hates you, Dan. He's hated you ever since you married Lane."

I laughed. It sounded dry, ugly. "He's got her now."

"Not before you spoiled her for him. You should have listened to me and never married her. Her parents didn't want you. She was out of your league."

"Maybe I should have listened to you, old friend. I remember your warnings about messing around with Margin's interests. But I loved Lane, and she loved me."

He shook his head, a sad smile on his lips. "You were always in love with danger, Dan. You still are."

"One more thing, Darl. What about the girls who were picked up for soliciting? Do you know what happened to them?"

His surprise seemed genuine. "Sorry, Dan. Nobody has been booked for soliciting. I'd know. There are no girls in jail."

I glanced at Killic. He didn't look happy. Then I showed Darl the picture. I knew I could trust him.

"What are you going to do?" he asked, shocked. "You're not going to leave her, are you?"

"No, my friend. We are going to find her, even if we have to tear apart this whole damned planet!"

Read the exciting conclusion in Book Two, Redemption.